# Patchwork

## A Collection of Short Stories

## Shelby June

Maat Publishing
Dover NH

ISBN: 978-0-9960302-9-8

Library of Congress Control Number:  2018935658

**Maat Publishing**
**1 Crown Point Drive**
**Dover, NH 03820**
**contact@maatpublishing.net**
**www.maatpublishing.net**

# Contents

# Behind the Glass

There is a certain amount of comfort in knowing when you're going to die. At least that's what I've told myself for the last twelve years.

I will not miss this bed, this inch-thick mattress, this flat pillow and the cement floor and walls. I have taken down the photos of my wife and daughter and placed them in a box, along with my journal, sketch pad, colored pencils and all of the cards and letters that they have sent to me over the years. This box will be given to my wife, Jocelyn, or "Jo" as I have always called her, and my daughter, Lily, who will turn twelve a few months after I am gone.

I put myself here. For twelve years I have brought nothing but pain and sorrow to my family, especially my wife and daughter. I am ready, more than ready, to end their pain.

The other guys here on death row, they will walk to the death chamber crying and carrying on about how this is unfair, how they are innocent but they are of poor circumstances and couldn't afford a lawyer to get them out of this place.

I am a man of means, or at least I used to be. I could have easily hired a crackerjack lawyer to get me out of this mess. I could have easily lied my way out of here. I am many things, but I am not a liar. I am, however, a stupid and selfish man.

I'm on death row. You don't end up in a place like this

for running a red light or stealing a pack of gum. You end up here when you make a horrible mistake and you don't stop yourself from doing something evil, even when your insides are screaming at you to stop.

I know I deserve to be here, but at the same time, cannot believe I am actually here. I have packed my things, because tonight, while the others on death row are sleeping, I will be moved to what's called the Death House. I will spend tomorrow, my last day, there.

As a teenager, I remember hearing about Angola. Some people called it "The Farm." I heard things like it was one of the most feared prisons, that it was once a slave plantation before it was turned into a prison, and Angola would either break a man, harden a man, or kill a man.

What is my life like here? Well, we here on Death Row are in isolation 23 hours a day. I am in a 7' by 10' cell. I have a stainless steel sink, toilet, and a metal mirror on the back wall. I have a table and stool and a bunk on the left wall. There are two pull-out drawers that are a part of the bunk and I also have two foot lockers.

Breakfast is served between 5:30 and 6:30 a.m., lunch between 10:30 and 11:30 a.m. and dinner between 3:30 and 4:30 p.m. Meals here are called "chow." It doesn't take the orderlies an hour to serve the meals, but they are brought to our cells on a tray. Everyone on the tier is served at once. Trays are picked up about 10 to 15 minutes after they are served so we don't have a lot of time to eat. There is a bulletin board on the tier with a menu for the week, but sometimes it gets changed without notice. Orderlies, also known as Trustees, bring the trays, and they also clean the tier and give us supplies to clean our own cells. They live across the parking lot at Camp F. Camp F consists only of Trustees, and most of them are serving life sentences.

I get four yard days a week (Monday through Thursday) for an hour. There are 10 individual pins side by side separated by a fence. One inmate per yard pin. You have to sign up for yard time. Someone usually comes around and asks everyone if they want to go out that day, and then we do on a rotating basis. When we come back in, we can take a 15-minute shower. I never miss a yard day, I love being outside. Friday, Saturday and Sunday there is no yard time but we have a tier hour where we can use the phone, take a shower, get ice or microwave things that we have bought. We also bring things to other inmates if they need it. All of us on the tier rely on each other to do things during tier hours, such as getting ice or doing some microwaving. Each tier has its own ice chest, microwave, trash can and mailbox.

I am so glad I can vividly remember holding Jo in my arms and even our last kiss. I think of those things every single day. I think of the night we met, all our times together, the day we got married, our honeymoon, buying our first house. I also think of the day that Lily was born. I hate myself for not being there with Jo. I was here in my cell, reading a book when Carl, one of the guards, came to my cell. "It's a girl," he said. "Lily Jocelyn Chapman. Ten fingers and ten toes - congratulations, man." I swear, I didn't stop smiling for about a month. Then Jo brought Lily to visit for the first time. That's when the reality set in – the reality that I would never hold my daughter, that I would never go to a father-daughter dance with her, attend her high school graduation, her college graduation, or even walk her down the aisle when she got married someday. I will never be a grandfather, because I will not be here when Lily has her babies.

That was the day I made a big decision. I wasn't going to fight. I wasn't going to appeal the conviction, the death sentence, any of it. I told anyone who would listen that I wanted this over as soon as possible. All that got me was psychological evaluations. This lasted for over a decade.

My death would allow Jo to find a real father for Lily, since she was adamant that there would be no divorce.

Jo and I met at a high school dance. She was with her group of friends, and I was with a group of my friends. For me, it was love at first sight. She had emerald green eyes, the most beautiful red hair, and freckles. So many freckles! She was a straight-A student, but she was so sweet, kind and confident. She worked hard for her grades, and it didn't matter how much homework she had, she didn't go out, or even go to sleep, until all the homework was done. That's just the way she was, and it paid off.

My thoughts are interrupted by the clang of the door. Every sound, no matter how small or insignificant, sounds like it's in front of a microphone. There is no peace in here, there is no rest. The clang of a door opening, someone sneezing or coughing, the televisions blaring night and day. It's hard to have complete thoughts because it is never quiet. Ever. Even in the middle of the night, there are noises.

I hear the door to the tier. I look at the clock and it's almost three in the morning and I know what's about to happen. They are coming to take me to the Death House. This is it. I'm finally out of here.

"Ryan, take care man," I hear behind me.

"Yeah, you too," I say without turning around. "Take care, John."

We, the guards and I, are quiet for a while.

"Carl," I say. "Thanks for being a good friend, man." The other guards look up at me. "I mean, he would let me talk to him. He wasn't an asshole to me, he just listened." One of the guards nods his head; the others just look at me and then look back down or out the window into the darkness.

"You're welcome, Ryan," says Carl. "As inmates go, you've been a decent guy. Never gave anyone any trouble. All the guys should be that way."

I give him a quick grin, as we have reached our destination. We get out of the van, and I know I probably won't see Carl again. "Maybe sometimes you could check on Jo, see how she's doing."

"I can do that Ryan," he says. "Don't worry about anything." He puts his hand on my shoulder, gives it a quick squeeze. "Everything's going to be okay."

"Yeah, thanks," I say. I can feel my heart pounding in my chest and sweat on my forehead as I walk into the small building.

The handcuffs are taken off after the cell door closes. I am told to get some rest. Rest? This is my last day – I don't want to sleep it away. It's about four in the morning now, and Jo and Lily should be here in a few hours. We will spend most of the day together.

My mind is racing, as there is so much I want to say to them. I've said I'm sorry so many times the last twelve years I don't want to spend my last day saying it again. They know I'm sorry. Jo has told me many times she's proud of me and that my worst act, the one that has brought me to where I am right now, is not what defines me. She feels this way because she's known me for so long. She knows my heart, she knows my mind, and she knows tonight I am paying the ultimate price for what I've done. I'm ready to pay because the truth is, I've never forgiven myself for what I've done. How can I ask the Moore family, my family, a judge, a clemency board or the governor to forgive me? I can't. I don't want their forgiveness because I don't deserve it. My in-laws are on the same page as me. My arrest, my conviction and my sentence was carried out twelve years ago. The last thing my father-in-law said to me was "You're already dead to me." I will never forget his face when he said that or what I said to him, "I wish that they would strap me to the gurney right now and be done with it." He didn't expect this answer, as his change of expression revealed. It was a combination of repulsion with the slightest twinge of respect. Then he walked away. A tall, proud, successful Christian businessman brought to shame, by me. The worst part is, Jack and I used to be very close. He welcomed me into his family, he was happy to give Jo to me on our wedding day, and especially overjoyed when he learned he was going to be a grandpa.

"Here you go," I hear behind me. It's a guard with a breakfast tray. It's seven already. Three hours have flown by; reminding me how fast this day is going to go. Jo and Lily should be here in a couple hours. My anxiety is making it hard for me to eat. I look up, and find a guard sitting outside my cell looking at me.

"Are you waiting for the tray?" I ask him.

5

"Nope, just doing my job," he says.

"I'm not going anywhere," I say with a slight grin.

"Suicide watch," he says, with no grin.

"Seriously? This is called the death house, right?"

"Just part of the procedure, part of the job." He opens his magazine, ending the conversation.

Over the last twelve years I have heard that many times, especially in the last few days. Even the Warden, when he asked me what I wanted for my last meal, after I told him I wanted fried chicken, mashed potatoes, peas, chocolate pudding, soda, and a glass of wine. Then I blurted out "How many times have you been through this?"

"Been through what?" he asks.

"Asking someone what they want for their last meal."

"Too many. I don't particularly embrace the whole 'eye for an eye' thing, but I do believe in the law. This here is just part of the job." He starts to walk away, but then turns back. "Sorry. No to the wine, but the rest is okay."

"I didn't really expect it anyway." Alone again for a brief moment, as the guard is down the hall talking to the Warden, my mind immediately goes to Jo. Clear as day, I see her in her wedding dress, her hair long and flowing, a crown of flowers, her mother's pearls around her neck. Her eyes are a little teary as she approaches me at the altar. Her father gives her a kiss on the cheek, shakes my hand, and finds his seat next to his wife. Ironically, I remember thinking 'this guy has a strong grip – he's a big guy. I'd never want to be on his bad side.' I let out a chuckle.

"Something funny? It's the guard sitting outside my cell.

"Just remembering," I say. He nods and goes back to his magazine.

We are pronounced man and wife, share a romantic kiss, and run down the aisle, hand in hand, laughing. Not exactly proper, but a whole lot of fun.

The reception was amazing. A huge white tent, full of pink roses, candlelight and 200 family members and close friends. There was a lot of laughter, dancing, great stories disguised as a toast, the fancy sit down dinner, our first dance, then –

"Chapman! On your feet. Your family is here." I look at the clock, it's 9:30 a.m. They're a half hour late. I'll let it slide; I'm not going to start a fight. Not today. The shackles are put on and I'm led to the visiting room.

"Dad!" Lily runs to me and throws her arms around me. Almost twelve years old and this is the first time this has happened. I look at Jo, and she has tears in her eyes.

"Hi, sweet girl. Let me look at you." She backs up and smiles at me. Her red hair is long, like her mother's, and she's wearing a navy blue, pink and white plaid dress. Jo is wearing a black skirt with an emerald green blouse. She looks stunning. They are both stunning. We all sit down at a round table.

"Tell me about school, honey. I want to hear all about it," I say.

"Our daughter loves school, she's doing so well," says Jo.

"Do you have a lot of friends?" I ask Lily.

"No," she says, "but I have a few good ones." She looks at her mother, and then at me.

"Few good ones are all you need," I say. Jo smiles at me. "Tell me about them, your friends."

"Well, we're in the same classes, we're in band together, we have sleepover parties, do each other's hair, we go to the movies sometimes, and we study together a lot. They're just ... nice."

"Very nice girls," says Jo. "They have a great time together."

"That's great, Lily. Friends are so important. I'm glad you have some good ones. How about school, how is school going?"

"I like school, Dad. English is my favorite class. We get to read a lot of books."

"Oh, yeah? What's your least favorite class? I bet I can guess."

"Math, for sure," says Lily. "I think it's really hard."

"She starts with a tutor next week," says Jo. "The school

7

has a buddy system where a high school student helps someone like Lily, who struggles with math."

I smile, because as usual, Jo handles whatever comes their way. I'm so proud of her for that.

"Why are you smiling?" asks Jo.

"You. You make everything better. You see a problem and you fix it. My super-strong Jo."

"It wouldn't be fair to Lily to be anything else," she says. "Tell your father about your new adventure."

"New adventure, what's this?" I ask.

"Well, I'm starting a new instrument soon," says Lily. "I am going to learn how to play the violin."

"Violin, really?" This is news to me. It must have just been decided. Jo didn't say anything about it before.

"I like the way they sound," says Lily. "Grandpa is giving me his violin, once I learn how to play it."

"Wow, that's very generous," I say, looking at Jo. "I didn't realize you were seeing your grandparents."

"I'm not, Dad. He called the house the other day."

"How often does he call the house?" I look at Jo, wondering why she's keeping things like this from me.

"He started calling about a week ago. He calls to talk to Lily, and as long as he doesn't bad-mouth you, Ryan, I don't mind him calling. He understands that the subject of you is off-limits and so far he is following that rule."

"We just talk about basic things, Dad. Things like school, and then when he asked if anything new was happening, I told him about wanting to play the violin. That's when he told me he used to play."

I smile and nod at her. Any other reaction would ruin the rest of the visit. "Your birthday is coming up, are you having a party?"

"My friends are staying over and we're going to rent some movies."

"That sounds like fun. Look, Lily, there's something I want to say to you. I'm sitting here, looking at you, how beautiful you are and so smart like your mother. I want you to know I'm so very proud of you. I know you are going to do great things, and I just – I just want you to keep me in your heart so I can experience everything you're going to experience right along with you. Will you do that for me?"

"We're both going to do that, honey," says Jo. "We promise."

"I can't ask for more than that." I look at them both, taking it all in. "I'm a very lucky man."

"How's work going, Jo. Did you sell the Maple Drive house?"

"We close in a couple weeks," she says, smiling. "I'm surprised it took that long to find a buyer. Young couple, recently married, they are so excited. Almost giddy. I think I found a buyer for the Preston house too, so things are going great."

"I'm proud of you, Jo." To my surprise, I start to tear up. I start to get emotional, and I was hoping that wouldn't happen today, but realistically, how could I not. This is my last visit with the two most important people. "I'm sorry," I say. "I'm so, so sorry for all this. For everything, for letting you down, for being a shitty husband and a shitty father. How could I do such a thing? So *stupid!*"

"No, darling," says Jo. "Don't talk like that. You made a terrible mistake, but that doesn't mean you're a shitty anything. You made a mistake. We love you, Ryan, you have to believe that."

"I love you, Daddy," says Lily and she wraps her arms around me. She squeezes tight, and I squeeze right back. How I will miss this; how I will miss them.

We talked and laughed and remembered; we talked of our wedding day, and of better times. Lily had questions about what was going to happen, which made her upset; she wanted to stay through the end but the rules state witnesses must be at least 18 years of age. That's one rule I'm grateful for. When our visit is through, Jo will take her home to stay with a family friend, and she'll come back for our final goodbye.

I hear the door open and a guard comes into the room. I

know what this means. "Sorry, Ryan. Time's up."

"Okay, man," I say. "Just a second, okay?"

"Time to go, ma'am," he says to Jo.

"Yes, sir," says Jo and tears fill her eyes. I know this is the hard part and I try to contain my emotions in front of Lily.

"Bye, sweetheart," I say to Lily. "I loved our visit today. Don't forget, take me with you in here." I tap my heart a couple times.

"I will, Daddy," she sobs. "I promise I will." She throws herself into my arms and holds me tight.

Jo hugs the both of us. "See you in a bit," she says to me and gives me a kiss.

"Okay, honey," I say. "I love you both so very much."

My shackles are put on and I'm led from the room. The last thing I hear is "I love you, Daddy," and uncontrollable sobs.

~~~~~~~~

An all-white room, with four large observation windows. That's what I've walked into. I am here to watch my husband die for a crime he committed a little over 12 years ago. He has always maintained his guilt, he never wavered. He never tried to get away with it or lie. And for that reason, other than loving him, I have stood by him all of these years.

The curtains open, and I see Ryan. He is strapped to a gurney wearing a white t-shirt and some prison pants that are cut off at the knees. He seems to be wearing slippers. At his waist band I see the hint of a top of a diaper. I close my eyes; Ryan must have hated putting that on. This place has so many rules and regulations; I know it wasn't his choice.

I see him scan the room with his eyes until they meet mine. I give him a warm smile and blow him a kiss. His lips turn up into a small grin.

"Any last words, Chapman?" asks the Warden.

"Yes, Sir," he says. "I would like to say something. I am so sorry for what I did 12 years ago; I have thought about that night every single day since then. This is the only way to even begin to show my sorrow and regret for what I did. Jo, I love

10

you and Lily so much, honey. I love you."

"I love you too, Ryan," I say as I walk up to the glass. I put my hands on it, and I continue to talk to him. "Ryan, don't you worry about a thing. Lily and I are going to be just fine. We will miss you every day, but we will be okay. We'll see you someday, my darling."

I don't know if he heard me but I stayed there, hands on the glass, as they started their procedure. He explained to me once what would go on today. There are three large tubes filled with three different drugs that will kill him. The guards press a button and the first tube starts to go through the IV. The first one is called Sodium Pentathol, which will put Ryan to sleep. The second, Pancuronium Bromide, a muscle relaxant that will paralyze Ryan's lungs. The third and final is Potassium Chloride, which will cause Ryan to have cardiac arrest. This should all take about 15 minutes, which it did. The flatlining alarm has jarred me from a short daydream. I think of our wedding day, me in my beautiful gown and Ryan in his tuxedo. That beautiful vision has carried me through the last 12 years and will carry me for the rest of my days.

It wasn't long after that beautiful day that our lives changed forever. Ryan was with three friends, Jack Thompson, Mark Riley, and Alex Winston. They were out celebrating Mark's upcoming wedding. Yes, they were drunk beyond control, Ryan has always maintained that. Jack became furious, and told Ryan and Alex that his wife, Melissa, was cheating on him. They drove to the lover's house, and banged on the door. There was no answer. They all went out in the back yard and before Alex or Ryan realized what was happening, the back of the house caught fire. Within a few minutes, most of the house was engulfed in flames. Ryan, Alex and Jack took off to another bar.

The next day on the news, the fire was a headlining story. Apparently, there was an elderly couple asleep upstairs who perished in the fire. I was in the kitchen baking and listening to the television. Ryan walked into the living room, and started to watch. "Oh, no. Oh my God. No. This is *not happening.*" He ran his hand through his hair several times and started pacing around the living room.

"Ryan, what is it?" I asked. I picked up a hand towel and wiped my hands. He continued to pace, saying "Oh my *God.*"

"Ryan, please tell me. What has got you so upset?"

"We did it. Jo, we set that fire. That's Melissa's boyfriend's house!"

"Ryan, no. Please tell me that's not true," I pleaded with him.

"I have to go to the police station," he said.

"What? Ryan, no. We need to hire a lawyer," I said.

"Hire a lawyer, but that's not going to change anything. I'm guilty. I was there, I helped kill two people. Oh my God, Jo. I'm sorry. I'm so fucking sorry!"

We went to the police station. Ryan was very open and honest and told all he remembered, which was just about everything, except the name of the last bar they went to. By then, he was too far gone to remember. I knew this bachelor party was a mistake, nothing good ever comes of them, but I had no idea something like this would happen.

The trial took two weeks, and the jury was out almost six hours before they came back with a guilty verdict. Ryan expected that so there was no surprise there. Because a crime happened during committing another felony, setting the fire, and the victims were both over the age of 65, Ryan was given the death penalty. I don't know what happened to Jack and Alex. Their trials were separate, and they both plead not guilty. I was four months pregnant at this time, and my only focus was being there for Ryan and taking care of myself and the baby. We named her Lily before we knew she was a girl, long before she was born.

My parents continuously begged me to divorce Ryan and live my life "the right way," which I refused to do. Daddy threatened to disown me, cut me out of his fortune, and I imagine he was furious when I told him to do whatever he thought he needed to do. I felt sorry for Ryan and what happened during that fire. Those poor people, dying in their sleep, not even knowing what happened to themselves. That poor family. Pregnant, knowing I'm going to be a single mother; I didn't feel sorry for myself. I was, and still am, a successful real estate agent, and I make plenty of money. In that respect, I am very lucky. Ryan's situation never bankrupted us or ruined my reputation as an agent. I am so grateful for that to this day.

I walk out of the prison, now a widow. My head is hung from the weight of the sorrow I feel. Ryan's funeral is the day after tomorrow; it has been planned for almost a year now. It will be a beautiful service and a wonderful tribute to my husband and Lily's father.

"So, you're finally free," I hear in front of me. I look up, and there stands my mother and father.

"Free?" I ask. "I don't consider myself *free*. A widow, but not free."

"Can we talk to you?" asks my mother. Her eyes are pleading, almost hard to resist.

"Why now, because Ryan is gone? That is supposed to erase the way you both treated me? No, I have nothing more to say to you."

I would like to thank Daniel Irish, Death Row Inmate #399680
Louisiana State Penitentiary
for his help with this story. This story is not about Daniel, but through his words he helped me understand the world he has lived in since 1996. At the time of this publication, he is still in the appeals process.

# No Longer for Sale

It all started with a crush, what I thought was an innocent crush. It was my first one, and it was a new boy at school, Justin. I wasn't overly pretty, but definitely not ugly. Plain, I guess you could say. I had a decent figure but hid it under LL Bean clothing.

I was shocked when Justin began to return my glances and smile at me in the hallways at school. He became friends with my older brother, Max. They played football together and would work out mornings before classes.

Justin was gorgeous. Dirty-blonde hair, athletic, smart, a little bit of a bad boy look, but very charming.

One night after a football game, a group of us went out to a club for some dancing and karaoke. We all had so much fun. Justin even asked me to dance, during a slow song. "Want to get out of here and grab some pizza?" he asked.

"Sure, why not," I said calmly, but on the inside I danced even faster.

"Max, Justin is going to bring me home, okay? We're going to get a slice and then I'll be home right after," I said.

"If you stay out too late, you're going to get in trouble, which means I'm in trouble too, so don't blow it," said Max.

"Don't worry, I'll probably be home before you," I said with a smile, and left the club with Justin.

We sat in the pizza parlor and talked and laughed. I was

smitten for sure, and I think Justin was too.

"I promised I would be home early," I said to Justin. "But this was really nice, thanks for the pizza."

"Sure, anytime," said Justin. "I think you're pretty cool. Someone I should hang out with more." His big smile melted my heart. "Let's go, don't want you getting in trouble because of me."

We went to his car, got in and put our seatbelts on. I directed him on which way to go to bring me home. We started to drive, and I was happy that Justin took his time. We continued to talk and laugh.

We were driving along a wooded area, when Justin began to pump his brakes. "What's wrong?" I asked.

"I'm not sure. I'm going to look under the hood. Stay here, I'll just check it out."

"Okay," I said. I began to feel a little anxious about the time.

Justin popped the hood and he looked around the engine with a flashlight. All of a sudden I heard another voice.

"Derek, what's up? Got something for me?"

"Sure do, man. Take a look." I see someone look around the hood at me, and then back at Justin. "Not bad, not bad at all." I see him hand Justin a bunch of money. "Nice job, my friend." The hood goes down and the stranger got into the driver seat beside me.

"Who are you? Why are you calling Justin Derek?" Before he answered I felt his fist against my face and everything went to black.

I don't know how long it was before I woke up, but when I did I was lying down on the back seat and blood was running down my bare legs. I felt very strange, not myself at all. Everything looked fuzzy and my head felt like it weighed a hundred pounds. I had trouble keeping my eyes open, so I finally closed them again.

The next thing I remember is waking up in a room with brick walls, a cement floor lying down on a bed with only a mattress, no bedding.

"Good, you're awake. Time to go to work." I looked around the room, and near the door stood a huge man, who wore jeans, a black t-shirt and a black leather jacket.

"Who are you?" I asked. "Where am I? I'm supposed to be home."

He chuckled. "This is your home now, get used to it."

I shook my head, "What?" My head started to feel funny and I felt nauseous.

"Here, this will make you feel better." He came at me fast and put a needle in my arm.

"*Drugs?* I don't do drugs! Are you crazy?" I tried to pull away but he only jammed the needle in harder, which made me cry out.

"Just a little something to help you," he said, and I felt myself falling asleep again.

"Thatta girl," he said with a smile.

The next time I woke up there was someone on top of me. *Oh my God, no. This can't be happening. I'm a virgin, I'm waiting until I have a husband!* "Get off of me! Get off of me!" I started to push and kick until he got off of me and stood up.

"What the hell, whore – we're not done until I say we're done!" He got back on top of me and kept going, until he was 'done.'

When he left the huge guy came back in and he was furious. I have never been beaten in my life, and I couldn't imagine what I looked like when he was finished. My whole body hurt.

"You will never disappoint a customer again. Do you hear me? Next time you won't be so lucky!"

"Customer? I don't even know what's going on here. The last thing I clearly remember is getting pizza with Justin, then someone called him Derek and took off with me in a car, then I woke up and you're here. Who are you? What did I do to deserve all this? Now I'm not even a virgin anymore. What will I tell my husband when we get married? I don't understand any of this!" I looked up at him, my swollen eyes pleading for him to tell me something. *Anything.*

"You now work here. You will have about twenty customers a day. I don't care what you're name used to be, it's now Diamond. If you tell anyone your real name, or ask anyone for help, I will kill you, do you understand? I hear everything, everything that goes on in this room, and if I hear anything other than a satisfied customer, I will fucking kill you, do you understand? That's all you need to understand, I promise you that. Here, clean yourself up." He threw a wash cloth at me, which I quickly put to my swollen face.

"What's your name – what do I call you?" I asked.

"You can call me Jack," he said.

"Where am I? When can I go home?"

"You are home now, and that's all you need to know," he said, and walked out of the room.

In the beginning, I would keep count of how many times I was raped. I stopped at 635 because the higher the number got the more depressed I got. I would look around my bare room and try to think of ways to commit suicide to get out of this nightmare, but it was so bare there was just no way. Sometimes, when I was getting my injection of what I now know was heroin, I would ask Jack to give me too much; just let me die and put me out of my misery. His answer to that was giving me more customers than usual that day.

One morning, Jack came into the room and told me I was leaving that day. I could hardly contain my excitement. Until he told me that I had been sold again. I was given a small bag of clothes and makeup to bring with me.

"Do you know where I'm going?" I asked. "Are you going with me?"

"I have no idea where you're going and I don't know who bought you, so don't ask. You're lucky I told you that much. I'm staying here, I have other girls to look after, not just you."

"How many are there?"

"Enough. There are enough of you whores to keep our customers happy, that's all you need to know. People get sold and swapped around all the time. You'll probably get sold again

17

after a while."

*This is sick, this whole thing is sick, I thought to myself. How the hell am I ever going to get to go home again? I'm never going to see my family again, am I? I wonder if they're looking for me ... God, please let someone find me!*

The next time I woke up, I was being dragged out of a car. I had a blindfold on, and if I looked down I could see my feet in some cheap flip-flops. I had no idea where I was but I heard voices.

"Very nice, I'll take her," said a deep voice. "Here you go, and let me know if you get any more. This is a good age, the customers like the younger ones, which I don't get, but they pay top dollar for them. Whatever floats their boat, right?"

"You got it Roy, nice doing business with you," said Jack. "I'll have Morris call you with any future offers."

"Definitely do," said the deep voice, and then there was a painful yank to my arm dragging me away to the next vehicle. Again, the jab of a needle put me into another deep sleep.

I woke up to more voices. "Get on the floor and put the blanket on top of you!" I did as I was told. I was still in a running car, but we were stopped.

"Good afternoon, sir, we are searching cars. Maybe you heard there was an Amber alert? Have you seen this girl?"

*Me? Was it me they were looking for?* I let out a groan since that was all I could manage, I was still so groggy.

"What was that, sir?" asked the officer.

"I'm taking my dog to the vet," said the deep voice.

I let out another groan, louder this time.

"Sir, step out of the car." I heard the door open, then close again. Then I heard the door near me open. The blanket was lifted off me.

"Dear Lord," said an officer. He had a kind, concerned face. *It's over. Please God, let this be over.*

"I need some help over here!" he hollered. He pulled the blindfold off of my face. "What's your name, sweetheart?"

"Diamond," I replied. My voice was a little slurred. "Are my parents looking for me?"

18

"I'm sure they are. What's your real name? It's not really Diamond, is it?"

"I'm sorry," I said. "I can't tell you. He'll kill me. Please, *please* don't make me tell you."

"Okay, that's enough questions for now. We'll have you brought to Memorial Hospital and have you checked out. The ambulance is here now."

I was helped onto a gurney and taken away. I fell back asleep in the ambulance, even though I was being asked questions.

I woke up in a hospital bed, and there were IVs in my arms. A nurse was taking my vital signs. I heard beeping coming from a machine, and people were coming in and out. I saw a police officer sitting outside my door.

"Why is he here?" I asked the nurse.

"For your protection. You have obviously been through a lot. A little security never hurts, right?"

*Where was this protection when I needed it the most?*

"My name is Jess, what's yours?" asked the nurse.

"My name is Diamond. How long have you been a nurse?"

"Almost ten years. You know, I'm pretty good at reading people. I bet Diamond isn't your real name, is it."

"I can't tell you my real name. I'm sorry, I just can't."

"I would love to call your parents, but I don't know who to call. Can you give me their name and number?" asked Jess with a smile.

~~~~~~

"Oh my God, it's really you!" gasped my mother as she ran into my room. "Oh honey, it's so good to see you. Let me hug you!" I can't remember the last time someone hugged me. I wonder how long it's been.

"Hi Dad," I said. He went to hug me but I cringed. I'm not ready to be touched by a man, not even him. Not even my father.

"It's okay, honey," he said. He stood at the foot of the bed.

"Mom, what day is it?" I asked. Being locked away with

19

no windows, no daylight, no moonlight, no sight of sun, dark or seasons I had no idea where I was at when it came to time.

"Well, it's Wednesday, honey," she said. She put some hair behind my ear and held my hand.

"But what day is it. The month, I mean," I said.

"Oh, it's Wednesday, April 20th."

Six months, that's it. Gosh, it seemed longer than that. "What year?" I asked, almost dreading the answer.

"Well, it's – 2016," she said as she rubbed my hand.

"2016? I've been gone *three years?* Oh my God!" I put my hands in my face and sobbed uncontrollably. I knew it was a while, but not years. I couldn't contain my sobs so I just let it all out. All the pain, the abuse, the violence, everything I had been through. "Did you look for me? Did you miss me?" I looked at my parents.

"Of course we did, sweetheart. There were search parties and posters and interviews on the news, newspaper ads, anything and everything we could think of," sad Dad. "Every single day we looked for you. Leah, you have to believe us."

"She does, Cal, she was just asking," said my mother as she brushed my hair. "She knows we would never give up on her, don't you honey?"

"I know. Three years is such a long time, I had no idea." The tears started to run down my face again. "I can't believe I got out of that alive." My parents looked at each other. "I don't want to talk about it," I said. "I'm not ready."

"That's fine, Leah. The important thing is that you're safe now and we can bring you home soon," said Dad. "God, it's so good to see you." There were tears in his eyes now, and he walked over to look out the window.

"I know Dad, I was just asking. I can't believe it – three years. I should be a Junior in high school right now."

"There is plenty of time to figure all that out," said Mom. "We'll figure it out, don't worry. You'll graduate; you'll do everything you planned to do."

"Ohhhh," I moaned. "My stomach." I held on to my stomach for dear life. The pain was intense. In fact my whole body felt in pain. My mother called the nurse. It turns out dehydration and malnutrition were the least of my worries. I was withdrawing from heroin. I was an addict, though an involuntary one.

The nurse explained to my parents my detox would be very intense and difficult for the next week or two. I believed her, but I certainly didn't want it in my system any more, nor did I want it there in the first place. My life became someone other than mine, the monsters, the thousands of monsters who mercilessly ravaged me and ignored my repulsion while they did whatever the hell they wanted. I wonder how many of them had daughters. I wonder what they would do if they entered the room of a prostitute and their daughter was there to greet them.

"You're going to get through this, Leah," said my mother. "We'll be with you every step of the way, honey."

"I didn't want to take it, Mom," I pleaded. "I didn't want it!"

"We know," she soothed. "We know you would never do such a thing on your own."

"Leah, just focus on getting better. You heard the nurse," said Dad. "It's going to be a rough couple of weeks, but you'll do it."

I gave him a weak smile, but on the inside I was screaming. My whole body hurt so much, I couldn't stop moving my legs and my thoughts were racing. I wanted to sleep so badly, but couldn't seem to keep my eyes closed.

This lasted for almost two weeks, and it was *hell*. I can't believe I made it to the other side. My parents kept their promise, they were with me the entire time.

One morning my parents came into my hospital room. "We have a surprise for you, sweetheart." From behind my father came my brother, Max. He looked so much older, I couldn't believe it.

"Hi, Max," I said. "It's so good to see you. You look so grown up."

"Leah – I'm *so sorry*. I had no idea Justin, Derek –

whatever his name is. I, I had no idea."

"Of course you didn't, Max. I have never, ever, blamed you for anything. All this time, you've been blaming yourself? That's just crazy, it's not true. None of this is your fault, Max."

"So you don't hate me?" he asked.

"No, of course not," I said. "Is that why this is the first time I've seen you?"

"Well, I had finals too," said Max. "I'm glad to have those behind me."

"Mom, has the doctor said anything about me going home? I've been here for weeks now. I'm really feeling good, I just want to go home."

"Well, actually," said Dad, "that's another reason why Max is here. We're all going home together. A road trip, maybe make a few stops on the way. What do you think of that?"

"That sounds great, when do we leave?"

~~~~~~~~

During the first few hours of our trip home I fell asleep. I woke up screaming. I imagine the nightmare of the last three years of my life will take time to leave my mind. My father pulled over, and my family comforted me the best they could.

Unfortunately, this happened a few times during the trip. My family was wonderful.

I don't know what is going to happen next, what my friends will be like, how I'll go back to school again, any of it. The only thing I know for sure is that I am no longer for sale.

# The Salad Bowl

*(Excerpt from "Lost and Found" by Shelby June)*

As I walk into the dining room for dinner with my family, I can't help but notice how beautiful the table looks. "Lydia, this is just beautiful!"

"Oh, thanks Aunt Nava," says Lydia. "There's just something about a set table that I just love."

"She thinks it makes the food taste better," laughs Isaac.

"Very funny. Don't listen to him, Aunt Nava," says Lydia. "He never complains about my cooking, and he better not start now."

"Come on now, sweetie," says Isaac, pulling Lydia into his arms. "You know I'm kidding, and you know I think you're amazing."

"Well, thank you. That's better," she says, and gives him a quick kiss.

Nina places a salad bowl in front of me. "Thank you, Nina." I can't help but stare at it. It is a small, round wooden bowl. The vibrant vegetables become black and white. "Move along!" An SS officer is glaring at me as I continue walking with my bowl of lukewarm "soup." It is raining and my ill-fitting clogs keep getting stuck in the mud, slowing me down.

"Mother? Mother, do you not want salad?" asks Olivia, and I come out of my daydream. Everyone is looking at me.

"Oh yes, I love salad," I say. I can feel myself shaking.

"Where were you just then?" asks Olivia.

"I'm right here. I'm fine," I say, trying to sound convincing.

"It's the bowl," says Malka. I look up at her and quickly shake my head, hoping this will make her stop. "It's the bowl and she's fine."

"I don't understand," says Lydia. "Would you like a different bowl, Aunt Nava?"

"What's going on?" asks Olivia.

"Everyone, please. I'm fine," I plead.

"In Auschwitz we used bowls like these," says Malka. "We guarded them with our lives. We carried them everywhere because you didn't get another if you lost it or if someone stole it. It's all we had to eat from and often time they were used for a toilet as well."

"Oh, God," says Lydia. She stands up. "Nina help me. Let's get these bowls out of here. I am so sorry, Aunt Nava, I had no idea. Hurry Nina. Please."

"Nina stay right where you are. Lydia, please sit down." She walks over to me. "Nava, this is a wooden bowl, but it's not that bowl. Okay?" She puts her hand on my shoulder and gives it a loving squeeze.

"Okay," I say. "Okay." I look at her and calmness comes over me like a fuzzy blanket. She smiles at me and walks back to her seat.

"Let's eat," says Malka, and takes a sip of her tea.

"Um, what just happened here?" asks Olivia.

"She's fine, Olivia. She has post-traumatic stress. She has hidden her feelings for so long, everything is a trigger, and everything will be until we do something about it."

"And what are we going to do about it?" asks Olivia. "Mother, I don't know what to say."

"Olivia, I have convinced your mother to speak to someone, he's coming to the house to talk to her. Tomorrow."

"Really? Mother, I'm speechless. I'm so proud of you, agreeing to talk to someone," says Olivia.

"I'm so embarrassed," I say.

An orchestra of "Don't be silly," "It's a great thing to do," and "Don't feel that way," fills the room.

"Aunt Nava, we're all here for you, and we'll do anything and everything to help you through this process," says Isaac.

"Amen to that," says Malka. "Let's eat. This all looks wonderful."

# Just A Few More

The cafeteria is crowded and noisy, a typical day at school. It has been a long morning of classes and I'm ready to relax and goof around with all my best girlfriends – Brit, Amy, Jen and April."Mya, has Bobby talked to you yet?" asks Brit.

"No, not yet," I say. "Has he talked to you?" I can't hide my disappointment. I've had a crush on Bobby for almost two years now.

"I'm going to ask him the next time I see him," says Brit. "I'll let you know what he says."

"Thanks, Brit. You're a good friend." We continue to eat our lunch, and Brit keeps looking around to find Bobby.

"You've had a crush on this guy for a long time," says Jen. "How come you've never talked to him?"

"Come on, Jen," I say. "You know I'm shy when it comes to guys. I'm not like you, but I wish I was. That's why guys fall at your feet." We all laugh. I have been friends with these girls since the first grade, and since April lives across the street, I've known her my whole life, but the five of us are like sisters.

I hear Brit gasp, "He's here. It's about time," she says. Brit gets out of her seat. I turn to look and she's standing right behind me facing away from me. "Bobby, come here!" she calls.

"Hi, Brit," says Bobby. "What's up?" I smile at his deep voice.

"I just wanted to ask you about something. I was wondering what you think about Mya. You know she has a crush on you, right?"

There is a brief silence. I'm certain he doesn't know I'm behind Brit. I hold my breath, waiting for his reply.

"Mya? I like Mya, she's great," he says. I let out my breath, smiling.

"You should ask her out, Bobby. You two would make such a cute couple," says Brit.

"I don't know. Mya's a great girl, but you know how it is."

"No, I guess I don't," says Brit. "What's the matter? Why won't you ask her, you just said she's great."

"And I meant it, I think she's great, I do. She's just not ... dating material. Not for me, anyway," says Bobby.

"I don't get what your problem is," says Brit. "You're not making any sense."

"Yeah, sorry. It's just that – well, she's smart, and funny, and fun to hang out with, you know? She's part of the group and everything but, well, she's just–"

"Just what?" asks Brit. I can tell she's growing impatient with him.

"I don't want to sound like a jerk, but ... I like skinny girls. Mya, well, she's not skinny."

"God, Bobby. Shallow much? Mya is not fat. She's beautiful, but you – you're ugly. Not on the outside, on the inside."

"Sorry, I'm just being honest," says Bobby. "I'll see you later." He walks away, and Brit sits back down next to me. She puts her arm around me. "This is why guys suck. You deserve much better, so forget that creep."

"Yeah, what a jerk," I say. I smile at my friends, and the conversation turns to afternoon classes and soccer practice after school.

~~~~~~~~~

"Hi honey, how was school?"

"Same as always, Mom," I say. I start to go upstairs, but she calls me back. "Yeah?"

"Dad's working late, I thought we could go out for

27

dinner tonight," she says with a smile.

"I'm not hungry, we stopped for pizza after practice. Plus I have a lot of homework." "Oh, okay. How was practice?" She opens the fridge and takes out deli meat for a sandwich. "Would you like a drink or anything?"

"Nothing, thanks. Practice was good, I'm a little tired and I have a lot of homework to do, so – "

"Always so conscientious, I love it," says Mom. "I'll let you get to it."

Happy to be in the privacy of my room, I peel off my soccer uniform. I stand in front of the long mirror that is behind my door and look at myself at different angles. He's right, I need to lose a few pounds. My stomach starts to rumble because there was no pizza after practice. I'll never get a boyfriend looking like this. I slip on my pajama shorts and a t-shirt and get started on the homework.

Several hours later there is a soft knock on my door. It opens and mom peeks around the door. "How's it going up here?"

"Good, I'm almost done," I say.

"How about a movie and some popcorn downstairs when you're done?" she asks.

"Do we have any fruit?" I ask. "I've got a craving for some grapes." I put my books in my backpack and place it next to tomorrow's outfit on my desk.

"Sure, movie and grapes it is," she says. "Coming?"

"Right behind you," I say as I turn out the light.

~~~~~~~~~

"New dress, Mya?" asks April. We're at the bus stop at the end of our street. "Looks great on you."

"Thanks, I did a little shopping with my mom," I say. "I get tired of wearing the same old thing, you know?" I won't tell her it's two sizes smaller. She doesn't seem to notice, anyway. I've got more work to do.

"Definitely, I do too," says April. "I swear that bus arrives later every day. I can't wait to get my license."

"Oh, I know. I've been hoarding my babysitting money

28

for years now so I can get a decent car when I'm old enough."

"How much have you saved?" asks April.

"Almost five thousand dollars."

"Seriously? That's great! That's a lot of babysitting."

"Babysitting, holidays, birthdays. I put it all in my savings account and I never take it out."

"You are so good with money. I spend all my allowance as soon as I get it, I'm terrible that way," she says.

"I spend my allowance too, but the other money gets put away," I explain. We look up when we hear the school bus coming.

"Finally! Any later and we'd be late for school." We both get on the bus and find our seats in the back.

~~~~~~~~

I'm at my locker, taking books out that I need to do homework tonight.

"Hey, Mya," says Jen. "Where were you at lunch today?"

"I got a pass for the library. I have a lot of homework so I wanted to get started during school so I'm not up half the night doing it."

"Well, we missed you. Are you going home now?" she asks.

"I still have a lot of homework to do, so yeah, I'm going home," I say and close my locker door. "I'll see you later, okay?"

"See you tomorrow, Mya."

~~~~~~~~

I'm lying in bed reading when I hear a soft knock on the door. I close my eyes and pretend to sleep.

"Mya, it's time for din–" Mom quietly closes the door, leaving me to rest.

~~~~~~~~

I run down the stairs and into the kitchen. "I'm running late, I can't believe I overslept!"

"Slow down, honey," says Mom. "You're right on time. Have a seat and have some breakfast."

"I need to get to the bus stop. I have to ask April about something for class. We're having a test today, and I don't

29

understand something." I start down the hallway towards the front door. "I can grab something quick at school, it's no problem."

"Be sure that you do, I'm worried about you. You look like you've lost quite a bit of weight this past month. You don't need to lose any more." Really? Yes!

"I'm fine, Mom. I haven't lost that much, only what I gained last winter. I've got to go, okay? I'll see you after school." I walk out the door. She noticed, it's finally working. After a couple of houses, when I'm out of Mom's sight, I start to run. Every bit helps.

~~~~~~~~

I'm sitting in the library at school, enjoying the quiet. I'm reading a book for English class, "Catcher in the Rye," and I'm taking notes as there will be a test on it at the end of the week.

"There you are," says Jen. "Mya, why don't you come to the cafeteria anymore?"

"I've had so much school work to do, that's all," I say. "I'm just trying to get everything done and maintain my grades."

"Look," says Amy. "I'm all about good grades and all that, but you have always had a lot of homework, you've always gotten good grades. You have not always skipped lunch, rushed home right after school and basically stopped hanging out with your friends."

"Yeah, are you mad at us?" asks April. "I never see you outside anymore, only at the bus stop in the morning for a couple minutes."

"I'm not mad at anyone, I promise." I shake my head in frustration. "I'm under a lot of pressure. I want to get good grades so I can be approved for the college prep classes next year. I want to apply for scholarships to help with college tuition. That's all, I'm not kidding."

"College tuition? That's like five years from now," says Amy. "You are putting way too much pressure on yourself and you need to stop." She grabs my arm, but instantly lets go. She looks at April and Jen. "What the hell, Mya. Jen, touch her arm."

Jen puts her hand around my arm. She looks into my eyes with complete concern. She opens my jean jacket. "Mya, what's going on with you? There is nothing to you."

April reaches over and lifts my shirt up a bit. She gasps, "Mya, what are you doing? You're not studying, you're skipping meals!"I look around the library. People are watching us and I can feel my cheeks warm with embarrassment. "Don't do this," I plead. "People are looking at us, let's get out of here." I walk towards the door, and behind me I hear a whisper, "What are we going to do about this? Should I call her mother?"

I swing around. "You need to promise me right now that you will not call anyone, especially my mother. If you're my friend, you'll keep quiet. I needed to lose a few pounds, so I have. That's it."

"Mya, is this about Bobby? What he said?" asks Jen.

"No way!" I leave the library. We are now in an empty hallway, and I'm walking towards my locker. My friends are relentless, so of course they follow me.

"How much weight have you lost?" asks April.

"I don't know, I don't have a scale," I lie. As of three days ago, I've lost over twenty pounds. "I just want to be more in shape, it will help with soccer and I really do feel healthier." Another lie – I feel weak most of the time, I have trouble sleeping so I'm constantly tired, I have trouble keeping focus in class, and my body always hurts. I have trained myself to tune out the rumbling of my stomach. Water has no calories, so I am constantly drinking that, I love it. It's the only thing I don't feel guilty about putting into my mouth.

~~~~~~~~

Walking up the street with April, I notice my father's car in the driveway. "That's weird," I say. "My dad is home early today."

"That is weird. He's usually not home until almost the time you eat dinner," says April. "Right?"

"Yeah, and sometimes even later than that. Well, see you tomorrow morning," I say and walk up my driveway.

"See you tomorrow," says April, and she walks up her driveway.

I walk through the front door, "Hi I'm home!" I look to my right and my parents are sitting in the living room.

"There's my girl," says Dad. "Come sit with us." Mom gives me a weak smile and it looks like she has been crying.

"Okay," I say as I put down my backpack next to the stairs. I collapse into the love seat and put a smile on my face. Dad home from work early, they want me to sit with them in the living room, weak smiles. This can't be good. "What's up?"

My parents look at each other and then at me. "I got a call today," says Mom. "It was Ms. Gregoire from school."

"Why would my guidance counselor call you? Is there a problem with the classes I chose for next year? Because I can handle the workload –"

"No, it wasn't about next year's schedule," says Dad. "Although, that is a different discussion for another time."

"Okay, so what's going on then?" I ask. I shift in my seat.

"How much weight have you lost?" asks Dad. "How many pounds, are you keeping track?"

"Just a few," I lie. "I'm not keeping track, I just want my clothes to fit better, and I want to do better at soccer, stuff like that."

"And how many more do you plan on losing?" he asks.

"Just a few more," I lie again. My friends, my best friends, have betrayed me. How could they do this to me? I will never, ever, forgive them for this!

"Take the sweatshirt off," says Dad. "Now."

"What? No way, I'm not going to do that!" I look at my mother. "Mom, tell him I don't have to, it's cold in here."

"It's not cold in here, Mya," says Mom. "Please just do what he says. We're so worried about you, honey."

"There's no need to be," I plead. I can't believe this is

32

happening. "This is not a big deal, I just wanted to lose a few pounds, what's wrong with that?"

Dad stands up and walks over to me. "Arms up, Mya." I put my arms up and he slides my sweatshirt off. I have a tank top on underneath. My mother gasps, and my father takes a step back. "Just a few pounds? Is that what you just told us a minute ago? No wonder you're always cold. There is no meat on your bones. How did we not see this? What have you been doing to yourself?"

"Mom. Dad. Yes, I've lost some weight, but come on, I needed to! I was overweight, and you can't deny that. I made some changes, good changes."

"You are a stick figure. A shadow!" When my father gets angry he runs his hand through his hair. He has done so six times in the last five minutes. My mother is on the sofa, crying.

"I'm not a shadow. You only think I look small because I was so fat! You guys are being so ridiculous! I'm going to my room, just leave me alone!" I run up the stairs, enter my room and slam the door. I start pacing back and forth. I can't believe my so-called friends. How could they do this to me? They're just jealous. Yes! That's what it is. Jealous bitches!

The next morning I intentionally miss the bus so I don't have to look at April's ugly, disloyal, back-stabbing face. My mother is more than happy to drive me. I tell her that every day the bus arrives later and later, maybe she could drive me every day? "Of course, honey. It's on my way to work. Ask April if she wants a ride too."

"I'd rather not, Mom." "Mya, she's one of your best friends."

"I know, but maybe I would like to just spend some time with just you." This makes my mother smile like I've never seen. "Is that okay?"

"Well, yes, of course," she says. "Wow, you just made my day!"

~~~~~~~~

Mom has been driving me to school for about two months now. I love driving by April who's standing at the bus

33

stop. I have had very little contact with Jen, Amy, Brit and April and I can honestly say I don't miss them one bit. I have been working so hard on my school work and my grades have been amazing. So amazing my English teacher is recommending me for Honors English next year.

"Where are we going?" I ask Mom. "This isn't the way to school. Mom, I've got class!"

"Don't worry, we're just making a little detour. School already knows you'll be late today and it's no problem."

"Of course there's a problem, my first class is math, and it's my most challenging class. You know that, Mom!"

"You just brought home an 'A' on your report card for math, so I think maybe, just maybe, you're overreacting."

"Mom, I got an 'A' because I didn't miss any classes and I worked my butt off for that 'A' so I'm not overreacting at all."

"We won't be here long, don't worry," says Mom.

"Wait – no way. This is my doctor's office. MOM, I don't have time for this!"

"Then we better get in there," she says as she gets out of the car. "Faster we get in there, faster we get out. Come on, let's go – I thought you were in a hurry."

~~~~~~~~~

"The last time you were here, Mya, your weight was 109. Your weight today is 88. Please understand our concern," says Dr. Foster. "Your parents and I are very concerned about your health. For your height and build 109 was below the normal weight range."

"That can't be right, because I was fat, so how is that below normal?"

"Mya, you're 5'4" so you should weigh between 114 and 127. That means you are at a minimum of 26 pounds underweight."

There is a soft knock on the door. "Come in," says Dr. Foster. My father walks in the room. "Sorry I'm late, I hit some traffic."

"No worries," says Dr. Foster. "I was just telling Mya she now weighs 88 pounds, and the normal weight range for her height and frame is between 114 and 127."

The hand goes through the hair. He looks at Mom, then at me. "I knew you were getting worse, but I didn't know it would be this – 88 Mya? I can't believe this." Hand through the hair again. "I want her admitted somewhere."

"WHAT?" I scream. "No way, I am not missing school!"

"That's something we can talk about –" says Dr. Foster.

"Today. I want her admitted today." He starts to pace around the office.

"Dad, I'm fine," I say.

"You are a liar! You lie to us constantly – 'I ate at school,' 'We stopped for pizza after practice,' 'I'll eat later.' It's all bullshit! You're killing yourself – right in front of us. No more, Mya. No. More!"

"Oh, my God," I cry. "This is not happening right now. Dr. Foster please tell them –"

"Mya, I'm going to step out with your parents for just a minute. We'll be right back." They leave the room. I take out my phone and I start a text to Brit, and then I remember there is no one to send a text to. What was I thinking, why would I ever send a text to those bitches? I'll deal with this myself, like I deal with everything else.

~~~~~~~~~

I walk down a wide carpeted corridor with my jacket in one hand and my suitcase in the other. I am following the intake nurse, Jane. She stops and motions to me. "This is your room, come on in." I slowly walk in, taking it all in. I notice that half of the room looks 'lived in.'

"Your roommate's name is Charlotte and I believe she's at a group session right now, but you'll meet her later. I'll take your bag, please." I hand her my suitcase and she opens it up.

"I can unpack myself, but thank you," I say. She looks at me and smiles.

"You will, in a minute. We always search belongings upon arrival, just part of the check-in process."

"But that's my stuff ..." I plead. Why won't she listen to me?

"Just procedure, we check everyone's bag upon arrival," she says and keeps looking through my things. I'm already irritated. I wonder how long I have to stay here.

~~~~~~~~~

"How come she doesn't have to say anything?" asks a red-headed skeleton. I'm sitting in group session, the first of the day. One session in the morning and another session in the afternoon. I have been doing this for two weeks now. I have nothing to say to these people. We have nothing in common. The red-headed skeleton is so skinny it's no wonder why she's here. I am still a little overweight and I'm here too? It makes no sense. She continues to complain how I never talk to anyone, 'blah blah blah' is all I hear her say.

"Why are you so concerned about what I have to say? You don't even know me!" I shoot back. More complaining. I hate this place!

~~~~~~~~~

"Mom, I want to come home. Now, please, I'm begging you. Please come get me, I can't stand it here one more day." I know I'm too old to be whining like this, but I'm at the end of my rope.

"Your father and I will be there for a visit on Saturday," she says. "We'll put a call into Dr. Sheldon before then and talk to him about how you feel."

"Great." Now we're getting somewhere. Saturday seems so far away, but in reality it's only three days away. Reality doesn't live in this place I can tell you that. Just a bunch of skeletons walking around trying to find ways to beat the scale so they can go home. One girl put things in her socks to add weight to her weigh-ins. Of course she got caught, she must think they're really stupid around here, but these nurses have seen it all I'm sure. I never try to pull anything, why would I? I'm almost at my perfect weight, just a few more pounds and I'll be happy. I think.

~~~~~~~~~

I've been here at Fairbanks for almost a month, and today is Family Day. My parents will be here soon. We will get a chance to visit, and then there will be a family session for the three of us. I wish Charlotte, who has become a good friend, could come with me, but that's not allowed.

Nurse Jan sticks her head into my room. "Mya, your folks are here, come on out." Oh boy, here we go.

"Coming," I say, and put my book on my nightstand.

At the end of the hall I see my parents. They look nervous but when they see me they are all smiles. I run into my father's extended arms. "Hi Dad, I'm glad you're here." I give my mother a hug too. "Hi Mom, thanks for coming to see me."

"We wouldn't miss family day, honey," she says. "How are you feeling?" she asks.

"You look great, honey," says Dad. "Can we visit somewhere?" I lead them to the community room where there is an empty table.

"Good turnout for Family Day," says Mom as she takes her seat. "Well, here we all are. The other day, Mya, you sounded upset. We put you here for your own good, we promise. Not to hurt you, to help you."

"I know, Mom. I've gained some weight, can you tell?" "I did notice, and we're proud of you, sweetie," says Dad. "You still have a way to go before you come home, but we're just – we're just so proud of you."

"Don't cry, Dad," I try to comfort him. "I'm okay. I'm going to be okay. I'm eating, I promise."

"Just don't stop," he says, sobbing. My mother takes his hand and gives it a squeeze.

"We've been so worried, Mya," says Mom. "Very, very worried about you."

"So how much more do I have to do? How many more pounds do I have to gain to get out of here?" I ask. I'm feeling frustrated, antsy, and upset that I don't get to leave here today.

"Just a few more," says Dad.

~~~~~~~~~

Family Day was a success, I got through my family session okay, and we made a game plan and set goals. I'm hoping to go home in about a month, as long as I meet my goal of weighing 100 pounds. I am at 93 today, and I am excited at the possibility of going home, getting back into school and making some new friends, since I still don't trust who I thought were my best friends. I try to think about them, try to forgive, but I can't bring myself to do it yet. Maybe someday, but not today.

~~~~~~~~

"That's it right? I did it, right?" I ask the nurse. I am standing on a scale and anxious for her answer.

"You know I don't tell you your weight, Mya, but yes, you did it." I hug her, I'm so happy. I get to go home! It took longer than I wanted but I finally did it. I can't help but feel exhilarated, even proud of myself.

~~~~~~~~

"I thought we could stop for some lunch on the way home, is that okay with you, honey?" asks Mom.

"Sure, that's okay," I say. Here we go, I'm being tested already. "Can we go to Friendly's?" This brought big smiles. I guess I passed the test.

I ordered my salad and Mom and Dad got their burger and sandwich. I started to pick at my salad when I noticed I was being watched. "I think I need some dressing after all," I say and Mom hunts down the waitress. She comes back with some dressing a couple minutes later. I start to eat and realize it tastes rather good, much better than the food at the hospital. After several minutes I actually finish the salad, croutons and all. You'd think I had just bought a winning lottery ticket the way my parents reacted. It's nice to see them smile though, I have to admit.

"Did anyone save room for dessert?" asks the waitress with a smile. Mom and Dad look at each other and then at me.

"I'd like a scoop of forbidden chocolate please," I say. More smiles. "Peanut butter cup sundae for me," says Mom.

"I'll take a banana split," says Dad, and we all laugh, because after a long time of struggle, lies and scary moments we finally feel the relief of the beginning of my recovery in the outside world, and so far, it's pretty bright.  I am excited for my future.

I think I'll call Jen when I get home.

# Boomerang

The parking garage was lit by only the moonlight. Stephanie was reluctant to try to find her car in the darkness, but couldn't stand out on the street all night either; money in the bank and not in her purse prevented a call to a taxi.

Cautiously and quickly she walked to her car. Nervousness made her slower, as she kept pausing to look around. Finally she saw her car, and relief overcame her.

When she put her key in the car door, she felt a hand come from behind and cover her mouth. "Don't scream, don't say a word, don't look at me," he hissed. "How long it takes, how rough it is and how much you get hurt is up to you. This is going to happen, so stop struggling."

He pushed her down to the ground and quickly got on top of her. His hand remained over her mouth until he put something in her mouth to gag her, then his hands held her arms above her head.

She continued to struggle and as promised, she was hurt. Anger inside her couldn't be contained. The hate rose and her struggle more intense. Over and over he hit her.

When he was finished, he spit on her. "You're such a slut. What do you have to say for yourself?" he asked. "Huh?" He glared at her.

She glared back at him, and adjusted her mouth after he took the sock out.

"Well, I asked you a question, slut. What do you have to say for yourself?"

She gathered the strength to smile at him. "I'm HIV positive."

# I Love You, Goodbye

I wonder what it's like for a doctor to tell a patient they have pancreatic cancer. I wonder how they feel when they tell you they can't operate, that there is nothing they can do other than help control your pain. This is what I'm thinking as my doctor tells me these things.

I have survived breast cancer. I will not survive pancreatic cancer. My thoughts quickly switch gears. How am I going to tell my husband? How can I possibly tell him I'm going to die? Then there's my parents. Devastation is the only word that comes to mind.

I walk down the corridor of the hospital towards the elevator. I wait for an eternity, it seems, for it to arrive. The doors open and the elevator is just about full, but room for me. Towards the back I hear a baby start to cry. I thank God I didn't have babies, because this would be so much harder if children were involved as well.

For over an hour I sit in my car in a daze. So many things running through my mind. I don't want to go home. I know when I look at my husband I will start to cry. He will start to cry, and we will hold each other until we fall asleep.

All of a sudden a thought pops into my head. A memory, really. I remember vividly looking at myself in the mirror the night I was told I was cancer-free, a little over five years ago. I made myself a promise I didn't think I would have to keep, ever, but I made it nonetheless. I promised myself that if I was ever diagnosed with cancer again, and it was incurable, I would move to Oregon and die on my own terms. It seemed crazy at the time, it really did. Now, not so much.

A wave of empowerment washed over me, and I started the car and headed for home.

I pulled into the driveway and parked next to Jackson's. He is not going to take this well, but he will take it because he has no choice. I have no choice. There are no choices here, this is our new reality. Somehow we will get through it.

"Hi honey," he says with a smile. "How was your day?"

As I predicted, I started to cry. "Well, other than having pancreatic cancer I'm doing pretty well. How was your day?" I have always been a blunt person, there is no way to sugarcoat this, and I'm not even going to try to.

I stare at him and wait for what I said to sink in.

"I think I need a glass of wine," he says. "I bet you could use one as well."

"You read my mind," I say and take a seat at the kitchen island. "I would love one."

As we sit and sip our wine, I decide to break the silence. "I'm sorry I was so blunt –"

"Please, blunt is your middle name," says Jackson. "I would expect nothing less. When do you start chemo?"

"No chemo. No treatment other than pain meds," I say. "This one is the big one, honey. I need you to understand that this time it's not a matter of me winning the fight, it's how long I can fight the fight."

"Come on now," he says. He puts his arm around me.

I pull away a little bit, but he squeezes my shoulder tighter. "I want to move to Oregon."

"Oregon, why would you want to move there?"

"I want to die on my own terms. I don't want to drag this out, I don't want to live in pain. Please support me on this. I'm begging you to let me do this my way."

"Well, how long –"

"Two years at the most," I say, knowing the question. "I'll know when I'm ready to move, I just need you to say –"

43

"I'll do whatever you want, you know that. I just can't believe this is happening." He pulls me into his arms and we walk to the couch. Again, as I predicted, we both cry until we fall asleep. I couldn't ask for a better husband.

~~~~~~~~

The next morning we wake up, and we are both grateful it's Saturday so we can stay home and talk and just be together. I'm sure we both look like we've been hit by a bus, but that's not the concern right now, obviously.

"Let's go for a walk after breakfast," says Jackson. We walk a lot together, and we love it.

"Sure, I'm up for it," I say. I know what he's doing. He's trying to keep things as normal as possible, and I am so grateful for that.

~~~~~~~~

"Jackson – hurry!" I scream. The pain is unbearable, I can't take it.

I hear him run up the stairs and he quickly enters our bedroom. "Here you go, take this," he says and puts a pill in one of my hands and a glass of juice in the other. "I'm so sorry, honey. I'm so sorry you're in pain."

I take my pill and give him a half-smile. He is trying so hard. With what little strength I have, I am trying too. Each day it gets harder to be brave, to be strong. Each day the pain gets worse, and Jackson and I dance around it, not talking about what we planned many months ago. The move to Oregon. I don't want to push him, but I know the time is coming when I will need to go. We will go together, we have searched the internet for apartments to rent for a few months. I don't know if I have a few months, to be honest, but I can't tell Jackson that. Not yet.

~~~~~~~~

"Honey, are you awake?" asks Jackson.

"Yes, I'm awake," I say with a yawn. It's the middle of the night, and neither of us can sleep.

"I think we should think about moving. I'm not trying to upset you, but I can tell you're in pain all the time. If you really want to go to Oregon, we should do it while you can still travel."

"Do you have any idea how much I love you? Any idea at all?" I ask. We hold each other until we fall asleep.

~~~~~~~~~

"I wish I could help you unpack," I say. I feel bad that Jackson does absolutely everything for me.

"You just sit there and continue to look beautiful," he says. "That's enough for me."

"We're so lucky we found a place that's furnished."

"We sure are. Need help into bed?" he asks.

"I'm okay here on the couch," I say. "I want to stay out here as long as I can, okay?"

"You call the shots, sweetie. Anything you need or want, you get." He leans down and kisses the top of my head.

~~~~~~

"Dr. Rosenthal, nice to meet you."

"It's nice to meet you too," I say. I don't have the strength to shake hands, but she gives my shoulder a little squeeze before she sits down on my couch. I'm in the recliner covered in blankets. It's so hard for me to stay warm these days.

"Dr. Rosenthal," says Jackson, "We've done a lot of research and reading about what happens and you come highly recommended. I'm so glad you had time to meet us today."

"That's great, that you've done research. The more informed you are the better," she says. "Do you have any questions?"

"No, you explained everything on the phone so well, I feel as though I'm ready. I'm happy to have some control on how I leave this life, I'm sure you hear that all the time," I say. I'm a little nervous, but Dr. Rosenthal has a very calming presence about her that I love. I know Jackson feels the same way. She spends hours at our apartment, explaining everything, about what is to happen when the time comes. She leaves the medicine with the instructions and pamphlets. She promises to return in a few days and for the tenth time, says if we need anything at all or have any more questions to call her,

45

day or night. I'm so glad I came here to Oregon.

"Thanks for coming, and thanks for your help and your patience," says Jackson to Dr. Rosenthal. "See you in a couple days." She gives me one last wave and walks out the door. "I like her a lot, honey."

"Yes, I do too," I say. "How about a shoulder rub? Just a quick one, please."

"Sure thing," says Jackson. "Whatever you need."

~~~~~~~~

"Jackson, I can't stand it. I can't stand the pain. I can't take it anymore. I just can't do it!"

"Honey, it's okay. I'll get your medication," says Jackson.

"Jackson. I think it's time. I'm getting worse. This isn't how I want you to remember me."

Jackson hangs his head. He knew this day was coming, he was just hoping for more time, I know. He stands up and goes to the kitchen. I hear him on the phone, calling Dr. Rosenthal for me. Thank God he understands.

"She's on her way," says Jackson. She said for you to take the anticemetic now if you're ready."

"What?" The pain has me a little unfocused.

"To prevent vomiting, remember? I'll go get it," says Jackson. I nod and he returns to the kitchen.

Soon there is a knock at the door. It's Dr. Rosenthal.

"Clair, how are you?" she asks.

"I can't take it anymore," I say through my painful tears.

"I understand. Do you remember all of my instructions? I wrote them down for you, remember?"

"I have them right here," says Jackson. He gives me some water and the medicine. He sits beside me on the bed and we talk of our wedding, trips we took, our families and the decision we made that brought us to this moment. Dr. Rosenthal was wonderful, she listens and laughs with us, and when we pause because of my pain, she holds one of my hands and strokes it gently.

Jackson begins to cry, and I do too. This is happening,

46

this is really the end. I am losing my battle of pancreatic cancer, but the end is here because I'm ready for it to be here. I want Jackson to have as many good memories as possible of our life together. I look at him and think about how much I love this man. "Please remarry," I say. "You can find love again, you just have to be open to it."

"Clair, I told you I don't want to talk about it," he says.

"Okay. Just know that you have my blessing when the time is right. I promise you have my blessing."

"Stop it, Clair. This is hard enough, I can't think about any of that."

"But it's what I'm thinking about, Jackson, and I just want you to know you have my blessing. And I want to thank you for the beautiful life you gave me. I love you so very much."

Through tears, he says, "I love you too, Clair."

I drink my juice filled with Secobarbital and we wait, we talk, we cry, we remember the good times. We hold hands, and I feel myself slipping away. It takes longer than I thought it would, but it gives me more time to look at Jackson. I look at him in his beautiful brown eyes and say, "I love you, goodbye." I close my eyes and begin my new journey. My pain-free journey, and it feels wonderful.

# Ghost Baby

Never before had I felt so alone. Two lines. Two lines that changed my life forever, because two lines meant that I was pregnant. Already a single parent to a two-year-old daughter, I couldn't put my family through another pregnancy. I was told after the first baby that if I ever came home pregnant again I would be out on the street. Remembering that statement did not make that decision any easier. I sat down and did the numbers. Could I afford to move out and raise two babies? Could I actually pull this off? I did the numbers three times and no matter what I crossed off the list to try to make it work, the answer was no.

Making the phone call to the clinic was heartbreaking. I cried through the whole conversation. There was a voice of an angel on the other end of the line. She was so patient, so nurturing and I didn't even know her name or what she looked like. She understood that I was making a choice that would allow me to survive. She knew it was a hard decision and she talked to me for almost half an hour, telling me it was going to be okay. "Just get here," she said, "and we will help you through this." I made the appointment for the following day.

The clinic was a busy place. The walls were covered with flyers and posters and the end tables were full of pamphlets full of information to make an informed decision. Getting into the building was the hardest part. There were protesters yelling at me, begging me not to kill my baby. They told me they would help me in any way I needed. Finally, I turned around and looked at them. I was about to yell back but decided not to. What good would it do? They had their beliefs and I knew I was making the right decision for myself.

I checked into the clinic and showed my license. After a short time in the waiting room, I was taken into a room and given an ultrasound to confirm how far along I was (eight weeks).

Next I met with a counselor named Amy. She was wonderful. She went over all my options and when I confirmed I wanted to terminate the pregnancy she thoroughly explained, step by step, the procedure and what to expect. The procedure, vacuum aspiration is used for pregnancies up to fifteen weeks. A cannula and a source of suction is used to remove the uterine contents. A local anesthesia for pain will be used. I am told it is an extremely safe procedure. I am told of the common side effects – abdominal cramping, pain, bleeding, nausea and sweating, and spotting for two to six weeks after the procedure. I signed the consent forms with tears in my eyes. Such an emotional day.

The next step was having some lab work done, and my temperature and blood pressure checked. So far, so good, everything was normal.

I was then given a pre-procedure antibiotic and led to another room to change into a medical gown. This whole day I have cried, even though this is my decision. It is the hardest decision I have ever made and will ever make. I think of the protesters outside, my baby at home, and those two lines. I think of tomorrow when I wake up in the morning, no longer pregnant, carrying a secret that will never be told to anyone but my friend Hannah, who was with me as my support system. She is a close friend and she will keep my secret.

In the procedure room, Hannah held my hand and told me everything would be all right. My thoughts and prayers for forgiveness drowned out the suction sounds. I thought of my baby at home, how much I loved her. I thought of my parents and the disgrace they would feel if they knew what was happening right now. I thought of the protesters outside with their posters with gruesome pictures on them, I thought of God and prayed for his forgiveness. I thought of my future – and then it was over.

"You did great," said the doctor. Hannah squeezed my hand. "It's over," she said with a half- smile. Such a good friend.

I stayed in the recovery room where staff monitored my vitals and bleeding for about an hour. I was then released to go home.

Even though the actual procedure was about fifteen minutes, I was at the clinic for almost six hours. I was emotionally and physically drained when I left.

Hannah brought me back to my car in my work's parking lot and I drove myself the rest of the way home. My family thought I was at work all day.

I walked into the house and was immediately asked by my mother if I was all right, since I "looked terrible."

"I haven't felt well all day," I said, and went to see my daughter. She was playing in the room we shared. She loved the collection of soft books she had and would look at them for hours. Her face lit up when I went into the room and she put her arms up for me to pick her up. I sat down on the floor with her and looked at her books with her.

After dinner, we played a little bit more until it was time for her to go to bed. We went to bed at the same time, and it felt good to lay down.

I closed my eyes and thought about the day. I couldn't believe I went through with it, that it was all over. I turned over and looked at my daughter, sleeping soundly, in her crib. I prayed that she would never have to make the decision I made today. I held her hand for a few moments and kissed her cheek, careful not to wake her up.

Twenty-six years have passed since that day, and whenever I see a baby I think of my own ghost baby, wondering what might have been if I had made a different decision. I know I made the right decision at the time, but that does not lessen the guilt that lives within me to this day.

# The Museum

*(Excerpt from "Lost and Found" by Shelby June)*

She stands at the glass, watching the video, the full loop, and then she moves on to the next one and watches that video. She walks very slowly, looking at every photograph, listens to everything she can. To look at her, she is in a trance. Sometimes she raises her right hand and touches the glass; sometimes she raises it to touch her face. If you watch her closely you would notice she doesn't blink for a long time. She is mesmerized by it all. Every so often another tear makes its way down her cheek.

It all sinks in, the experience. The uniforms, the trains, the soldiers, the barracks, the gas chambers, the piles of the dead. It absorbs her like a sponge, the words, the pictures, the countless black and white faces.

She can sense I am beside her but she doesn't turn to look at me. "She lived through all of this, Tim. She went through all of this. They both did."

I put my arm around her. "Yes, they did, and they survived it," I say.

"How?" She turns to me, her face tear-stained and pale. "How did they get out of that alive?"

"I don't know, sweetheart, I just don't know." I rub her back, relaxing her.

"Mom, are you okay?" asks Alex.

"She's fine, son, just a lot to take in," I tell him.

"Where's Grandma and Malka?" asks Abbie.

"I'm not sure," says Olivia. "Malka took her somewhere to show her something." She glances at her watch. "That was quite a while ago. Maybe we should go look for them."

"No," I say.

"No? Why not?" asks Olivia.

"Because they're fine. We're here with you now. Are you fine?" I ask her.

"I'm okay. Like you said, it's a lot to take in." She looks back at the glass at some photographs.

"What are you thinking right now, Liv?" I persist. "What's on your mind?"

"I'm the child of a survivor. I never really understood what that meant until now. I get it. I get it now."

"What do you get, Liv?" I need to hear the words.

"Why she did it, why she came here to America. Why she wanted to start over as a completely different person. Why she kept her secrets for so long. I don't know how to explain it, I just ... get it."

I smile at her, relieved, knowing she had to come to this on her own, in her own time. The past few weeks have been hard on her, but now things would be different. I have been with her long enough to know how to handle her, how to have the right amount of patience. Looking at her now I can see my "Liv" has come back. The softness in her face has returned, the tension lines in her forehead and cheeks have vanished.

"What are you smiling at," she asks me.

"My beautiful wife, that's who," I say.

# Slice of Heaven

I knew what kind of night I was going to have by the way my father arrived home. See, we have a dirt driveway, so if I didn't hear him drive up, I knew he was in a good mood and we would have a great night as a family.

If I heard him, by his speeding up the driveway and then slamming on the brakes and parking hap-hazzardly, I knew it was going to be bad. These nights I would stay in my room. When I was smaller, I would hide in my closet but he would always find me. Now I do homework or read a book. He doesn't bother me much if he thinks I'm doing homework.

My mother isn't so lucky. He will scream at her and I've heard him hit her many times. I hate the sound of her cry, and I hate that there is nothing I can do to help her. I tried once and my father raised his hand to hit me but my mother blocked me from him and took the blow instead. Later, when we were alone she told me that no matter what I heard to never try to help her because it only made things worse. She made me promise not to interfere, no matter how much I wanted to. That was the hardest promise to make.

I confided in a friend, Tracey, of what my home life was like. Turned out she had the same situation at her house. I felt awful about that but relieved at the same time; I realized that I wasn't completely alone.

"How do you deal with it, what goes on?" I asked her.

Instead of telling me, she showed me. She took out a

tiny razor blade and started making small cuts on her upper arm.

"Doesn't that hurt?" I couldn't believe what I was seeing.

"No, it actually makes me feel better," she said. "You should try it. Don't cut too deep though, just the top of your skin."

"Really? It makes you feel better?" I asked. I was very confused by this, had never seen anything like it before. I did want to feel better, but how does cutting myself do that?

"I don't know if I can do that," I said.

"Here, take this. If the time comes when you need it, you have it," said Tracey. "If you don't want to use it, don't. It helps me, maybe it will help you."

~~~~~~~~

Turns out Tracey was right, it completely took my mind away from what it was hearing – the screaming, the hitting, the throwing of things. I was cutting on a regular basis, four or five times a week.

One night, my dad arrived home in a hurricane. I knew it was going to be a bad night, and I was right. He came through the door screaming at my mother. He tried to call her from work and she didn't answer. A big no-no. She tried to tell him she went to the grocery store, but that did not help at all.

I went in my room to work on homework, but I couldn't concentrate. I could hear the beating, and mom was crying, he kept yelling and I prayed for her, I really did. Then I remembered Tracey once again. I took the blade out of my backpack pocket and sat on the floor in my closet, crying. Again, it helped me. Making the small cuts made such a difference, I really did feel better.

All of a sudden my bedroom door flew open, but it wasn't my father who stood there. It was a policeman. He looked at me and seemed to know what I was doing, and he made me give him the blade. I didn't want to, finally finding something that calmed me in all of this chaos I call my home life. He led me out into the living room. My mother was on the sofa, she had a black eye and a bloody nose and lip. She was crying and didn't look at me.

"I swear I didn't call them, Mom," I said. She nodded.

"Where is Dad?" I asked.

"He's being brought to the station," said the policeman. "I think you should tell your mother what you've been doing in your room."

Mom looked up immediately. "What's he talking about?"

"Don't worry about it, Mom. You have enough to worry about. It's nothing."

"If it was nothing, he wouldn't have said something. Come over here and tell me what's going on."

I rolled up my sweatshirt and showed her the little cuts on my arm.

She closed her eyes. "What the hell is going on here?"

"Ma'am, your daughter was cutting herself," said the policeman.

"Why would you do such a thing? How long has this been going on?"

"I have a friend who does it and she said it made her feel better. She has – the same thing happens at her house, that's why she does it."

"Oh my God," said Mom. "You have to stop, honey. How long has this been going on? It's not the first time, I can see some scars. How long?"

"Mom, I can't live like this. You can't either, it's not right," I said, crying. "I can't take it anymore, listening to him beat you, scream at you all the time."

"I asked you a question, young lady. You tell me right now how long you've been doing this. Now."

"A couple months, you know, whenever Dad goes into his tailspins," I said, looking at the floor.

Mom looked me in the eye and said, "We're leaving, honey. Your grandparents are on their way to get us. Go pack some things, okay? They will be here soon."

"Are you serious? We're leaving this place? Promise?"

"I promise. But you have to promise too, no more cutting," said Mom.

"You keep him away and I'll stop," I answer.

The policeman suggested counseling for us both to help us through, and suggested getting a restraining order, which my mother agreed to do.

For the first time in a long time, I felt a little better about our future. I felt so helpless, all those times listening to her being hurt so badly. When she looked me in the eye and said what she said I knew she meant it. The problem was him. It was always him. Will the restraining order keep him away? Will he leave us alone? I knew we would have a decent shot at my grandparent's house because they turned against him a long time ago. He knows better than to mess with my grandfather.

"Thank you," I said to the police officer. "I don't know who called you but I would thank them too if I could. You probably saved her life tonight," I looked at my mother.

"I have a feeling you were saved too," he said and tipped his hat.

# Not So Unsinkable

Richard and I were sitting in our stateroom when it happened.

"My, what was that?" I asked.

"A shudder, my dear," said Richard.

I went to put my tea on the coffee table but another shudder tossed the teacup from my hands. "Oh, goodness. How clumsy."

All of a sudden we heard loud voices in the hallway outside our room. Then there was a knock on our door. It was a deck hand. "Mada, Sir, please put on your life jackets and quickly go to the first class deck."

"What's going on?" asked Richard.

"I have to instruct more people," he said. "Please, just do as I ask."

"Yes, of course," I said. I go to get our life jackets.

"Put your coat on first," said Richard. He helps me put my long coat on, then the life jacket, and then I put my gloves on. He did the same, and we made our way into the hallway and followed the others.

I couldn't help but think about what life was like just a couple hours ago. We were in the dining room; we ate oysters, poached salmon, filet mignon, creamed carrots, rice, peas, new potatoes, roast squab, asparagus vinaigrette, and then finished the delicious meal with Chartreuse jelly, chocolate eclairs, waldorf pudding and fruits, nuts and cheese. How it melted in our mouths, it was simply lovely. The food, the music, the company. I will never forget this night.

Out in the hallway there were people running, shouting – the fear was undeniable. Out on the deck it was even worse. However, throughout all the chaos we could hear the calming sounds of an orchestra. God bless those men, they played beautifully as people ran past them to safety.

"Women and children, please! Women...and children ..."

They started to fill the lifeboats, only they didn't. Richard helped me onto a lifeboat, and the boat wasn't even half full when it started to lower down the side of the ship. As the lifeboat lowered I was able to grasp just how big it was – the ship was 11 stories tall.

I stared at Richard deeply into his eyes as the boat was lowered. "Richard, my love. Please find me again, my darling."

"You are going to be fine, my sweet wife," he said with half a smile. "I adore you." That's what he always said, instead of 'I love you,' he would say 'I adore you.'

Richard and I were going to visit his family in New York City. It was a surprise second anniversary present he gave to me. It was at this reunion I was going to share a special and wonderful secret with the family.

"We should go back," I heard from behind me. "This boat isn't even half full, and there are still so many people left on the ship."

"We cannot go back, they will overwhelm the boat and we'll sink," I hear someone else reply. I don't turn around, I stare at the ship. The front of the ship is so close to being underwater. I see people running around, people being loaded onto the lifeboats and to a small amount of joy; I still hear the orchestra playing. *Richard, you must survive my love, you are going to be a wonderful, loving father.* I rest my hand over my belly. *I wish I had told you, I shouldn't have waited.*

Quite suddenly, there was a shift in the ship, the front was completely under, and people were running to the back of the ship, which seemed to be lifting somehow. Never in a million years would I ever think I would see such a sight. Never in a million years would I ever think I would be separated from my husband in this way. Never in a million years ...

Screams of people in the water, splashing in the water, I will never forget this sight, these sounds.

The electricity on the ship started to flash; I put my hand to my mouth. *Richard, where are you? Are you on a boat, are you one of the figures I see hurrying to the back of the ship?* My darling ...

I began to pray. I closed my eyes and just prayed and prayed. For Richard, for everyone on that ship, and for everyone in the water, I prayed.

I could hear a high-pitched smashing noise. "What is that?" I hear someone behind me say. "It sounds like dishes breaking," is the response.

The back of the ship began to rise, so much so people start falling. Not just straight falling, as though they are diving into a swimming pool, but falling and bouncing off of guard rails and other objects. The sound of impact made my eyes squint. Again, I touched my belly. *Sweet angel, I hope we will be all right. I pray your father will be, too.*

The electricity on the ship flashed again, and then went completely out. The darkness was eerie, scary, and overwhelming, as the screams got louder and more intense. The ship split in half, and the noise of it as it came apart was deafening, it overcame the screaming we could hear. I know these sounds will haunt my dreams, perhaps forever. *How is this happening? How is this possible? This ship was called the ship of dreams, it was called unsinkable!*

The back of the ship is now standing tall, the screams continued, people falling continued, I prayed even harder at this sight and these sounds. *Richard, are you on a boat? Are you in the water? Are you hanging on for dear life? My darling, this cannot be our ending.*

The back of the ship, just a moment ago standing tall and proud, began to sink. It seemed a slow dissension at first, and then sped up. *Oh, Richard.*

60

It was at that very moment, I knew he was gone. My prayers turned to Richard being at peace, and to not suffer. The love of my life, the father of this growing child. He will be remembered, not replaced.

# Liar Liar

"I have a crush on you," he said. He looked so eager, so proud to say it. "Do you have a crush on me?"

"Yes," I said, immediately regretting the word.

"Great," he said. "Let's get back."

See, Shawn's wife Jackie and my husband, Randy, were at the movie theatre getting tickets while Shawn and I went to Best Buy to look at routers for my computer at home. We have all been hanging out for over a year now, but Shawn, Jackie and I all knew each other in high school and were friends back then. During high school Shawn and I were close friends but we were both dating other people. Who knew that those feelings would return 25 years later? I had no idea.

At that time, I wasn't really happy in my marriage, and Shawn wasn't happy in his, or so he said. I knew I would never cheat on my husband, and I had no intentions of doing so with Shawn, or anyone else for that matter. But a little flirting ... what harm would that do? I couldn't help but feel flattered, a little special even. I didn't know it would ruin a friendship that I had really come to love with Jackie. I came to love her as a sister, and here I was flirting with her husband.

From the time I said "Yes" about the crush, I felt awful. The guilt was eating me from the inside out. During the work day I would get flirtatious emails from Shawn. I would try to reply in a non-flirtatious way. I didn't want to hurt anyone's feelings or make things worse. Again, the guilt I was feeling was awful. I knew I had to stop this before anything went any further.

One day I was at Shawn and Jackie's house and I realized I had forgotten my allergy medicine. They had a couple cats and I was highly allergic to them. I told Jackie I was going to run home and get my medicine and return right after. Shawn said, "I'll go with you, Randy says your computer is running really slow and I told him I would look at it."

"Okay," I said, knowing this was a lie. I didn't say anything because I thought I could use this time to tell Shawn this all had to stop. The flirting, the emails, everything.

I didn't go home, I didn't want to be alone with Shawn in my house. He had this look in his eye and I knew he would make a move. My intention was to go to the pharmacy and buy the allergy medicine, even though I had plenty at home.

We stopped at a place called Hilton Park so we could talk. We ended up sharing a kiss.

"You look disappointed," said Shawn. I was. I was so disappointed in myself for the kiss. If Randy had kissed someone else I'd feel so betrayed. Even though I wasn't happy in my marriage I didn't want to hurt Randy, and this kiss made me realize I wanted to work on my marriage for real, to try to rekindle the feelings that I once had for my husband. That's what that kiss did, it made me see Randy in a whole new way.

Shawn on the other hand, was furious. I think he expected me to have sex with him, in my car, in broad daylight at Hilton Park. The guy is insane, and really a dirtbag for actually wanting to cheat on his wife, my best friend. I saw Shawn for what he really was for the first time and I did not like what I saw.

"I'm not cheating on Randy," I said. "Not with you, not with anyone."

"You don't love him," said Shawn.

"I never once told you that," I said. "Am I living in marital bliss right now? No. But that doesn't mean I'm going to sleep with you. I couldn't do that to Randy and I couldn't do that to Jackie either. Ever since that night at Best Buy I have felt so guilty. Don't you?"

"Not at all, I can't help the way I feel," said Shawn.

"Maybe not, but I can stop this all right now, and I'm going to. You and I will never be anything but friends. I'm going to work on things with Randy, and hopefully we can be happy. If we don't make it, it won't be because I cheated, it will be because we've grown apart and can't make things work."

"This is such bullshit," said Shawn.

"I'm sorry you're mad, but that's the way it is. Maybe you should work on your marriage too."

"Whatever, let's go back."

"Yeah, let's go back."

That's the last time I saw him. After that he told Jackie that I tried to lure him to a hotel room and wanted to have an affair with him (among other things, I'm sure). I lost my best friend because of his lies. To this day, six years later, I feel badly about what happened. Jackie hates me, has told her friends that I tried to be a homewrecker and sleep with her husband.

I told Randy everything. He actually understood, and he even apologized for letting our marriage take a backseat to everything else. Even though I lost a couple of friends, my marriage is in a better place that it has been in a long time. I still think of Jackie and I miss her, but I know that our friendship will never recover from Shawn's lies. I wish she could see him for what he really is, but that is for her to figure out on her own.

I am grateful for the friends that I have that would never think of hurting me that way, that value our friendship and don't cross any lines. I'm a happily married woman with many things to be grateful for, that's for sure.

# Sweet Caroline

Even though I've been fostering for over twenty years now, I still feel nervous anticipating the arrival of a new child. Will the child like us? Will I be able to help the child adjust to our home from the separation of their own home? Will this be the one child I can't help? This afternoon while I'm waiting for Caroline to arrive, I am anxious.

Finally, the doorbell rings and I run to answer the door. I open it with a big, welcoming smile on my face. There were two social workers, Linda and Monica, and they are standing on either side of Caroline.

"Hi there. I'm Andrea, come on in, please." Caroline walks right in and the social workers followed.

"This house is a lot nicer than my house," says Caroline. "My house is small ... and very dirty."

"Come here in the living room everyone," I say, leading the way. "There is some lemonade and cookies here for everyone."

Caroline takes a glass of lemonade and takes a big sip. "This is good," she says. However, when she puts the glass back on the coffee table, the glass slips out of her hand onto the floor. The glass breaks and lemonade spills.

Caroline covers her ears and runs into the corner of the living room. "I'm sorry!" she says over and over.

I look at Linda and Monica. I go to the corner and take

Caroline's hands off of her ears. "Caroline, don't worry. I know it was an accident. It's okay, really." I go to the kitchen to get some paper towels. The spill quickly goes away, but Caroline is still crying. "See? All better now," I say. Caroline calms down a little bit. I give her an unreturned hug.

I think of the file I read on Caroline. Severe neglect, physical and emotional abuse is all she has known so far in her life.

I look at her clothes, filthy dirty, faded and unmatched. I know a new wardrobe will be needed and internally promise myself to take care of that in the next day or two.

Linda and Monica begin to get ready to leave. "Caroline," says Linda, "Andrea's house is nice and clean and warm and has lots of nice furniture. You'll even have your own room here. There is plenty of food here and hot water too." I'm guessing that Caroline's house didn't have such things. Caroline gives a small smile.

"Can I see my room?" she asks.

"Of course, it's right upstairs," I say.

"Caroline," Linda says, "Monica and I are going to leave now. Andrea has our number if you ever want to call us, and we'll be back in a few days to see how things are going, okay?"

"Okay," says Caroline. "See you in a few days." Caroline looks a little sad, but at the same time is excited to see her room upstairs. We say our goodbyes for now.

"Well then," I say. "Let's go look at that room of yours."

"Okay," says Caroline, and she runs right up the stairs. When she reaches the top she turns around and waits for me.

We walk down the hall, Caroline is walking right behind me. "Here it is, this is your room. I hope you like it."

Caroline opens the door and the hallway immediately fills with the sunshine coming in through the windows in Caroline's room. It's a large room with pale yellow walls, a full-size bed with a white and yellow floral comforter with several pillows and new stuffed animals on it. On the far wall, there is a small table with coloring books and crayons on it. There is also a bookcase with several books, puzzles and toys on it.

Caroline stands in the middle of the room slowly taking it all in. "This is really my room? I don't have to share it with anyone?"

"It's all yours, sweetheart. And everything in it is yours too. Tomorrow morning we'll go to the store and get you some new clothes and shoes. Doesn't that sound like fun?"

"New clothes and shoes? Wow. I usually get hand-me-downs from the neighbor. I don't think I've ever had anything brand new just for me."

My heart is breaking for this little girl. It's one thing to read her file, but to see her face and hear that little voice is very real. She is my saddest case to date, I'm certain.

"Thomas, Luke and Marissa will be home soon, they've been at the park this afternoon. Then we'll all have dinner together. Luke is ten, and Marissa is eight, the same as you. I know you'll all be good friends," I say, hopeful.

"Who is Thomas?" asks Caroline.

"Thomas is my husband. He took this afternoon off to go to the park with the kids and to meet you."

"He has a job? What does he do?"

"He is a professor at the university. He works very hard so I can stay home with you kids."

"That's nice. My dad doesn't work. He stays home and drinks beer all day."

Again, my heart breaks. "That doesn't happen here, Caroline. Don't worry about that."

"Okay." Caroline walks over to the bed and touches the comforter. "This is so pretty. I can't believe this is all mine!" She runs up to me and gives me a big hug. I am so happy to bring a little happiness into her life, but I want her to feel loved in this house, not just enjoy material things. That is so much more important.

"Hello – we're home!" we hear from downstairs. It's Luke, making his usual loud and grand entrance. In moments, Thomas, Luke and Marissa are standing in the doorway.

"Well hello everyone, this is Caroline. She's checking out her new room."

"Hi, I'm Marissa. You look like my age, how old are you?"

"I'm eight," says Caroline.

"Me too!" says Marissa.

We make our way downstairs to the kitchen and Thomas and I start dinner. "I hope everyone wants hamburgers and hot dogs on the grill. I'm making a salad as well and we'll have ice cream for dessert."

"What's ice cream?" asks Caroline and instantly everyone stops what they're doing to look at her.

"Oh, well, ice cream is a delicious treat. I think you'll like it very much," I say, trying to hide my shock. Luke and Marissa are so shocked they don't say anything at all. Thomas gives me a look, but I just smile back at him.

It's so nice outside we eat our dinner out on the patio. Caroline enjoyed her dinner and even had two helpings of salad. She didn't say so, but I'm pretty sure that was the first time she had ever had it.

"Time for ice cream!" says Luke. "I want a big bowl of chocolate please, with chocolate syrup and whipped cream. My favorite."

"I think we'll all have that tonight," I say. Thomas and I clear the table. In the kitchen he whispers, "What's ice cream? Where has this kid come from?" I smile at him and say, "She's here now, that's all that matters." He nods in response.

I carry a tray out to the patio with the ice cream on it. Caroline's eyes grow wide and her smile fills her entire face.

"Wow!" she yells. "This looks amazing!" She takes a bite. "From now on, all I want is ice cream – nothing else!"

"Ice cream is a treat, Caroline. I hope you will enjoy all the food you have here. Sometimes we go out to a restaurant to eat, usually once a week. What foods do you like?"

"Well, I eat cereal and sandwiches," she says.

"What else do you eat?" asks Marissa.

"Once at my grandmother's house I had tomato soup, but just that once."

"You'll have all kinds of things here," says Luke. "Mom is a really good cook."

"Why thank you, son. That's nice of you to say. Why don't you guys play in the yard for a while, and then it's bath time for everyone, okay?"

"What's a bath?" asks Caroline.

"How do you clean yourself?" asks Thomas.

"With a wet towel, how do you do it?" asks Caroline. We all look at each other, once again.

"In a little while, I'll take you upstairs, Caroline, and you'll have your first bath, okay?" I say. This little girl has so much to learn.

The kids play outside for a little while and seem to enjoy each other's company. I'm so happy that things are off to a good start.

"The water is nice and warm, let me help you in the tub," I say. I take her hands and lift her into the tub. She looks so tiny in the large tub, I have to chuckle. "How does that feel?"

"This is nice," says Caroline. "Now what do I do?"

I hand her a facecloth. "Let's add some bubbles." This makes Caroline laugh. "Use your facecloth and wash yourself all over really good. I'll shampoo your hair."

"Mama uses a bar of soap, not shampoo," says Caroline.

"We use shampoo and conditioner here," I say. "I think it's better for your hair."

"Okay," says Caroline. "It sure does smell good!"

After her bath, Caroline ran down the stairs. "I smell good!" she yells.

"You must feel really good," says Thomas.

"I do! Can I watch television for a little while?"

"For about half an hour, then it's time for bed," I say.

Thomas turns on the Disney channel and the kids sit on the sofa together. I can't believe how well things are going so far.

"I've only watched television a couple times at my grandma's house," says Caroline. "We had a television at home, but my dad busted it when he was mad one time."

"Well, we're careful with our things here. Things don't get broken very often," says Thomas.

"You don't get mad?" asks Caroline. "You don't yell and scream and break things?"

"No, of course not," says Thomas. "That's not the way to express your anger, Caroline. There are much better ways to express your feelings than to yell and scream. Yelling and screaming only makes things worse, not better."

"I guess. My mom and dad yell all the time. They hit too."

I think of all the bruises I saw all over Caroline's little body when she was in the bath. I didn't say anything, but I certainly saw them.

"We absolutely do not hit in this house, Caroline. You never have to worry about that."

"Okay," says Caroline. She slowly looks around the house. "I like it here."

"We're glad you do," I say. "I hope you stay with us a long time."

"Me too!"

"Tomorrow after we bring Luke and Marissa to school we'll go shopping for some new clothes for you. You will start school on Monday."

"I hope I make some new friends. I don't have any at my other school. Kids would pick on me because my clothes never matched and they were always dirty."

"I'm sure you'll make lots of new friends, Caroline. You're such a sweet little girl. Luke, Marissa it's time to go up to bed. Everybody upstairs," says Thomas.

"Andrea. I have to tell you something," says Caroline. "Sometimes ... well, sometimes I wet the bed."

"Not to worry, I have a special cover for the mattress and I don't mind washing your sheets. You let me know right away if you have an accident. Even if you have to wake me up during the night, okay? I really don't mind."

"You really won't get mad? Promise?"

"I absolutely promise, Caroline. It takes a lot to make us mad, you'll see."

"I'll be good, I promise I'll be good," says Caroline.

It took several months for Caroline to stop wetting the bed. There was a lot of sheet washing during that time, but I kept my promise and didn't get mad.

Caroline thrived in school, and she made many new friends. For her ninth birthday, we had a big party for her at the house, and fourteen of her friends came over to celebrate. Caroline was beyond excited.

After over a year of living with us, we discussed the possibility of adopting Caroline. She has turned into a beautiful, well-behaved little girl who thrives at our house, and at school. She enjoys everything we do, from swimming to hiking to dancing around the living room. She loves to read, watch movies and even does her homework without a fight. She actually loves school and has made many friends.

One day, after almost two years of living with us, I found a note in our mailbox. It wasn't stamped, just left in a plain envelope. I carefully opened the envelope.

*"My name is Judy and I am Caroline's birth mother. I ain't no creeper or nothing but I watch your house sometimes at night when the lights are on and I can see in. I see Caroline and she looks real good. I see she got some new clothes they look real nice on her. I guess I should thank you for that. I never had any money to buy her nice new things like that. I've seen her dancing around in your house with the other kids. You got a real nice family and you seem to love Caroline. Don't think I don't love her too cuz I really do. That's why she's with you. I love her but I can't take care of her. Not the way you can. At first I was angry cuz you got a real nice house and real nice cars and you wear nice clothes. You have stuff I ain't ever had. Stuff I can't give my kids or even myself. Anyways I've been thinking about it. I think you should take in Caroline on a permanent basis. Cuz well I think she's better off with*

*you and your family. Caroline looks like she's real happy and already part of your family, so I just wanted to let you know it's okay with me, you know, if you want to make it official or something. Me and her daddy we talked about it and we will sign whatever papers we need to that will make it official. Well that's all I guess. I just wanted you to know that. Thanks for taking good care of my girl. If she ever asks you tell her we did this because we love her we aren't mad at her or nothing. Judy"*

"My mother wrote that?" asks Caroline.

"She did," says Thomas. "What do you think?"

"Well," says Caroline. "I guess it's more important what you guys think. Do you want me to be your daughter? For real?"

"Yes, of course we do," I say. "That's why we're having this family meeting. It's something we should all talk about and decide together."

"I vote yes!" says Marissa. "You're like my sister now anyway, right?"

"I guess so," says Caroline with a smile. "Luke is quiet, do you want another sister?"

"You've been my sister for a couple years now," says Luke. "I vote yes too."

"Well, it's official then," says Thomas. "I'll call the lawyer in the morning and we'll get the process going."

"How about a celebration?" I ask. "Dinner out tonight, and a huge party when the adoption is official."

"I'm so excited!" says Caroline.

"We're all excited, sweetheart," I say. Finally this little girl will be *my* little girl, and she will have the family she has always wanted and really deserves.

# Finding Him Again

I was raised in a loving, Christian home. I attended the Congregational Church in town, and when I was fourteen, I gave my life to Christ. I was active in the church and I invited friends from school to attend with me. I was also very open with my faith and talked to anyone who would listen about the love of Christ and the need for Him in their lives.

When I left home for college, I still attended a church on campus, but as each month passed, I attended less and less. I was discovering other things – partying, drinking, and even more than anything else, sex. By the time I was twenty-one, I had completely dismissed my faith, becoming an atheist.

Years after I graduated college, events began to take place around me which through the luxury of hindsight now, I can see were gently nudging me in a certain direction. The company where I worked hired a woman who happened to be a Jehovah's Witness, who began talking to me about her faith as a Witness. Still an atheist, and with my upbringing as a Christian, I started searching the Bible just to show her she was not only wrong about believing in God, but she was also wrong by believing such a bastardization of scripture. I was reading the Bible again.

One day, I called a client of our company that was a ministry for gang members who were trying to leave their gangs. As I entered the waiting room to meet the head of the ministry, at the reception desk sat a young girl who had all the markings of a gangbanger. Tattoos on her hands, bleached hair with dark brown roots, I could sense this was a girl who just yesterday could have been scoring drugs on the street or taking on multiple partners back at the crib. As I approached her, I fully prepared to talk to her. She looked up at me, and there was a gentleness and quiet peace about her that took me by surprise. She politely, quietly, asked me who I was there to see and if I would wait a moment while she notified him I was there. She asked if I wanted a cup of coffee or tea, and if there was anything else I needed, just let her know. I was blown away.

I spent the rest of the day thinking about her and asked myself over and over – What could cause such a change in someone? Government programs wouldn't make this kind of change, I reasoned. Radio talk shows featuring pop-psychology were such that I couldn't imagine them having such an impact on someone. I couldn't get her out of my mind.

The following week was a turning point. My daughters were then 3, 5, and 7 years old. Even though I was an atheist, I had become an atheist after first having a Christian foundation and then made the decision based on what I thought was all of the available information. I was very uncomfortable about raising my girls without offering them the same opportunity.

It was the winter of 1998, and I was in the field calling on accounts for my company when I got a call from my boss. He informed me that he didn't have all the details, but he had just gotten a call that my wife and children were involved in a car accident. He told me where to go, and I immediately hung up the phone and got into my truck. I looked up to the sky and said "Please, Lord. Let them be all right." Here I was, the big atheist, and in what I perceived as my darkest hour, I asked God to make my family safe.

When I arrived at the scene, my family was nowhere to be found. However, the other car involved in the crash was being attached to the wrecker and I was horrified to see the entire front end of that car crushed to the fire wall. The female driver of that car was in the back of the ambulance on a stretcher with her neck in a brace and IV's running into her arms. I again asked God to please make my family okay.

I found a policeman and asked him if he knew where the other car involved in the accident was. He told me that he was the second policeman to arrive on the scene, called in to wrap up the accident report after the first patrolman was called away. He told me that by the time he had arrived, the other car was already gone. I asked him if it had been towed away or driven away. He said he didn't know. I identified myself as the husband and father of the passengers in that car, and he gave me a business card for the police department. He told me to call the police station for more information. Not knowing what to do, I got back into my truck and headed back to my office.

All the way to the office I talked with God. I was praying and offering God anything in exchange for the safety of my family. As I drove down the long driveway, I saw the family car parked in front of my office. For the life of me I couldn't see a scratch on it. As I got closer, I was able to find a couple places that showed the force of the impact, but nothing that was noticeable from about twenty feet away. As I stared in disbelief at my car, especially after what I had seen of the other car involved, the front door of my office flew open and my wife and children ran out to hug me. Everyone was in perfect shape without one scratch. I held my wife and cried, and held my girls and cried some more. Right there and then I recommitted my life to God. I found a church and that Sunday rededicated my life during the service, as did my wife.

I understand now that the meaning of God's love for us is greater than any atheist's debate points. As they waste away their lives away over meaningless minutiae, the bigger picture that is God escapes them. The greatest truth that I have learned since I have come home again is that all of the arguments and debates in defense of an atheist exist for one reason – to justify sin. The reality is that, although I wanted to present my atheism as the result of learned, intellectual

75

inquiry, the realty was that I was just defending my choice of refusing God and living a sinful lifestyle. The only way that I could justify getting drunk, getting stoned and having indiscriminate sex, was if there were no absolutes railing against such behavior. By proving that God didn't exist, thereby rendering the Bible and all faith meaningless, I was then justified in doing my own thing when I wanted, how I wanted, where I wanted and with whom I wanted. There is not an atheist out there right now who is not doing the exact same thing.

I'm so glad to be home again, so grateful that I found Him ... again.

# Welcome Home

I knew from a young age that I was not wanted. My parents were not like other parents. They were cold and distant not only with me but with each other as well. The day they told me that they were getting a divorce I was not surprised, and even hoped that things would get better now that Dad was moving out of the house and into an apartment. I was not surprised when I was at the grocery store with my mother a month later that we saw him with another woman. They were obviously more than friends. My mother didn't say anything, but she had that look that said "I knew it." We continued shopping in silence. My mother never said a word about what we saw and I knew better not to ask questions.

Much to my disappointment, but not complete surprise, things did not get better between my mother and I. She was still distant and uninterested in my schooling, or anything about me for that matter. When I graduated high school many years later my graduation present was a suitcase. It was time for me to make it on my own, she said, and I was to find either a job or a way to put myself through school, immediately. I had a month to figure it out. One night I counted my babysitting and gift money that I had saved for the past four years, and to my surprise I had quite a bit of money. I had no idea how much anything cost, such as rent or utilities. My savings of a couple thousand dollars would not last very long, but it would help me get started.

I got a waitressing job at the town diner, Jake's, working the breakfast and lunch shifts so I could take some night courses. On the outskirts of town there was a rooming house where I rented a room. It was neat and clean and this one room made me very happy, though a little lonely. People at the rooming house kept to themselves and it was very quiet. Everyone was expected to keep it that way – neat, clean and quiet.

I had two friends from high school that I saw every once in a while but in the fall they went off to college. I was literally on my own. In a way, I was happy and proud of myself for building this little life for myself. In another way, I was sad that I was forced to leave my childhood home so soon. Sometimes loneliness would get the best of me, and I found myself getting lost in a library book when I wasn't working on schoolwork. My mother never called me, not once. If I saw her at the grocery store she would barely acknowledge me beyond a "Hello." She never asked where I worked, where I lived, what I was doing, how I was, or anything. One night she came into the diner with a man, but sat in another waitress' section. I saw her look at me but she didn't speak to me, and certainly didn't introduce me to her friend. He probably didn't know she even had a daughter.

I stopped asking myself what I did wrong a long time ago. My parents were just not meant to be parents. I am grateful they gave me life, but not grateful for the life they gave me. Whatever I had, I had because I got it myself. I would scrimp and save for whatever I had, even simple things like a new pair of shoes or a magazine. I promised myself that one day when I was married and had a child they would never feel unwanted. They would know how loved they were, they would see me in the front row at their school play, or at the bus stop ready to walk them home from school, they would never wonder if they were wanted or not, ever.

It took me four years, but I earned an Associate's Degree in Paralegal Studies. The law had always interested me, and it was my dream to work in a law firm. The day after I received my diploma, I went to the library to use their computer to create a resume and some cover letters to send out to local firms. I crossed my fingers that someone, anyone, would want to give me a chance. I didn't want to be a waitress forever, that's for sure, though the staff at Jake's had been wonderful to me and very supportive of my studies for a long time now.

Two weeks later I arrived home to a message on my answering machine, "Hello, this message is for Stephanie. This is Linda at Wallingford and Drisdale. I received your resume recently and would like to schedule an interview. Please call me back at your earliest convenience." I did a dance all around my room I was so excited. It was after eight that night when I listened to the message so I promised myself I would call first thing in the morning.

The next day I went to Goodwill and bought some clothes appropriate for the interview scheduled for next week. Could things finally be turning around? Years of struggle and hard work might finally be paying off. For a moment I thought about calling my mother, but thought better of it. I heard she moved out of state a couple years ago, without even telling me about it, so why bother. Times like this I wished I had someone special to share news like this with. This is when the loneliness would settle in. While I was at Goodwill I found a journal for only a dollar so I splurged and bought it. I told my journal everything, and it actually made me feel better. I even a little less lonely.

*Dear Diary – I got the job!*

I was so nervous my first day of work, but the people at the firm were so welcoming and patient. We started slow, teaching me the basic ways of an office such as how they want their phones answered, where the office supplies are kept, where my desk is located, where to hang my coat.

I wrote everything they taught me down and studied it at home. I didn't want to ask repeated questions or make mistakes, I really want this job to work out and stay a long time. Maybe save enough to get a real apartment, not just a room.

*Dear Diary – Six months at my job at the firm and it's going great. I have almost enough money to get an apartment, I can't believe it! I celebrated my anniversary by buying myself a new outfit. Did I mention I was given a raise? Life is good!*

When the new paralegal, Barry, started at the firm I finally realized what "love at first sight" really meant. He wasn't the most handsome person I had ever seen but he was handsome to me, and he seemed very kind. My first impression, other than baby blue eyes, was he was very polite and soft-spoken. He was shy, like me, and I liked him instantly. To my surprise, he seemed to like me too. A very nice surprise!

*Dear Diary: He asked me out! We're going to dinner and a movie this weekend. I'm so excited and nervous at the same time. I wonder if I'll get my very first kiss!?!*

*Dear Diary: I got my kiss! It was AMAZING!! Dinner was delicious, and the movie was really good. What a night, I hope he wants to see me again ... He even insisted on paying for everything, I couldn't believe it. He's an amazing person, I want to call him my boyfriend already! I hope he likes me too ...*

Have you ever had a string of good things happen, felt like you were on top of the world, and all of a sudden wondered if it was all going to be taken away?

*Dear Diary: You're not going to believe this, but Barry asked me to marry him. He proposed to ME, I can't believe it! We've only been dating for six months but I love him and he loves me so I just had to say ... YES!*

"Charlotte, I have something to ask you and you can say no if you want to," I said to my co-worker and now close friend.

"Sure, what is it?" she asked.

"Be my maid of honor?" I show her my ring finger and she lets out a yelp of some kind. I'm sure all the dogs in the neighborhood are awake now.

"Seriously? I want all the details – and of course I'll be your maid of honor!"

*Dear Diary: It was a beautiful wedding! It was small but very romantic and intimate. Our honeymoon was spectacular. We went on a cruise to the Caribbean, thanks to*

*Barry's parents. That was their gift, I couldn't believe it! A cruise!! More like a floating city, it was HUGE and I've never eaten so much in my life. We saw some beautiful islands – St. Thomas, St. John, St. Maarten and St. Kitts. I'll never forget it as long as I live!!*

"Are you ready Mrs. Johnston?" asked Barry. I am blindfolded and very curious about what he's up to now.

"I'm ready, can I take this off now?" I can't wait!

"Okay, take off your blindfold," he said. We were standing in front of a white house with green shutters with a white picket fence. "Well, what do you think? Do you like it?"

"It's from a fairy tale," I said. "What are we doing here?"

"Welcome home, Mrs. Johnston, it's our very own house. Surprise!"

"Our own home? Are you kidding me?"

"Like I said, welcome home," and he gave me the most romantic kiss.

# I Saw You

I was in a cab, stuck in traffic of course, waiting to get to your office building. I wanted to surprise you and take you out to lunch. Before children, we would have lunch a couple times a week. I miss that, so I was able to get a sitter for a couple hours. Then I saw you. I saw you … and her. And she was beautiful. Long, blonde hair, long tan legs, red fingernails, wide smile, eyes looking up at you. The same eyes that I look into. You look at her different than you look at me. You look at her with admiration, you look at me with appreciation. There is a difference.

You admire her beauty, you appreciate what I do for you. Clean your house, raise your children, and cook your meals. You appreciate me. You admire her. There is a difference.

"Sir, I need to go back to where you picked me up, please," I say to the cab driver.

"Yes, ma'am," he says with a confused look.

Back at the apartment, I thoughtfully and carefully pack your things into your suitcase. I'll even let you have the good luggage. Why not? I'm sure you'll *appreciate* that.

I put the luggage outside the door a few minutes before I expect you home. I stand on the other side of the door, listening. I listen to the children chatter as they eat their dinner. I listen to the quiet hallway and wait to hear the elevator door open.

All of a sudden, it does.

"What the –" I hear you say. I smile. He knocks on the door. I open it, leaving the chain on so it only opens a few inches.

"What's going on, Connie?" he asks. He looks concerned.

"I saw you," I say. He closes his eyes and takes a deep breath.

"I saw you," I say again. He nods, picks up the suitcase and goes back to the elevator.

As the door of the elevator closes I hear an "I'm sorry, Connie," but I say nothing. He is sorry he got caught, that is all.

I close the apartment door. "I'm sorry too," I whisper. "I'm sorry I saw you."

# My Last Breath

Standing in the cattle car I knew where I was going. I heard the rumors throughout the ghetto after my family received notification that we were being sent away from the ghetto to a "better life" of work and better housing. As I stood there holding my infant son, Isaak, and squeezed against my two daughters, Malka and Nava, I knew exactly where we were going. I didn't tell my girls of course, I couldn't do it, though Lord knows I tried a few times.

My husband and I would exchange glances when we could; he was crammed against a wall of the cattle car and amongst some of our neighbors. We stood like this for days. *Days.*

I sat on a bench while my hair was being shaved. Just a few minutes before an officer killed my infant son, Isaak, because he was crying. Broke him in half like he was some kind of stick and threw him on the ground. I died right along with him. My hair fell to the floor and I only thought about my daughters and their beautiful long hair. Nava would be heartbroken; she loved her hair so much. Malka would be a little upset but I know her and she would say "It's only hair, it will grow back." My twin daughters are alike and so different in many ways.

Standing naked in the 'showers' I knew what was coming. This was not a shower, this was where I was going to die. On the wall there were what looked like scratch marks, people trying to get out maybe. I thought of my husband, my son, my daughters. I started to pray – pray that my daughters would survive this and find each other so they could take care of each other.

That is how I spent my last breath. I prayed.

# Unfaithful

The first time I saw her I was mesmerized, almost hypnotized. She was the most beautiful woman I had ever seen, by far. Green eyes, long, dark hair and even longer legs. Fitted blouses and pencil skirts with high heels and just the right amount of makeup and jewelry. She was a vision to say the least. Right away, I noticed there was a huge wedding ring on her finger, but I couldn't help the way I felt.

"She's married," taunted my co-worker, Chris. "And by the way, so are you."

"I know, but she's just so ..."

"She's so married," repeated Chris.

"She's coming this way."

"Gentlemen," said our boss, Matt. "I want to introduce our new Vice President of Marketing, Leah."

I stood up quickly and held out my hand. "Welcome to the team."

"Thank you, and you are ..."

"Jason. Jason Montgomery. Nice to meet you."

"You as well," she said with a smile. Hypnotized.

"Well, you blew that," said Chris after Leah and Matt walked away. "You acted like she was a celebrity or something."

"She's a vision," I said, watching her make her way around the office.

"I have never seen you like this," said Chris. "I'm not

sure I like it, under the circumstances. Forget it man, you would never cheat on Lizzie, you guys are such a great family. Think of the kids for crying out loud. You remember your kids, right?"

"Of course I remember my kids. And I remember Lizzie. Don't be ridiculous, but I just can't take my eyes off of her. We better get back to work."

"Smartest thing I've heard you say all day," said Chris, laughing.

The next day was no different. Leah was in my sight and on my mind all day. When she left for lunch with the marketing group, I actually felt disappointed, almost jealous. I wished I was part of the marketing department – something before now I would never have imagined. I loved being part of the finance team. Numbers have been my life for the past twenty years or so.

Still, my mind wandered. *What was her husband like? Does she have children? What is she like outside of work?*

"Snap out of it," said Chris. "What are you thinking about? As if I didn't know. Dude, you need to stop this."

"I know. Just wondering about her life, you know? What's she like outside of this place? What's her husband like? Does she have kids, how old are they? Maybe they go to the same school as Jake and Tessa. Stuff like that."

"It doesn't matter. You have your own life, man. I can't believe you're doing this. Yes, she's extremely hot, but she's not worth losing what you have."

"I haven't done anything, Chris. Stop your worrying already."

"I am worried. I was at your wedding. I was at your kids' baptisms. We take vacations together. Of course I care about what's happening right now. I'm trying to be a friend here, you know, help you out of this mess. No, you haven't done anything physical, but it's like you're having an emotional affair, which isn't fair to Lizzie, Jake or Tessa. You know I'm right, don't you?"

"Look, I know what you're saying, but what's happening here ... it's harmless, really. It's just me fantasizing I guess."

"You guess? How would you feel if you found out Lizzie was fantasizing about someone else? Wouldn't you be upset? Feel betrayed?"

"No, I wouldn't. She can fantasize all she wants as long as she comes home to *me*."

"That's bullshit and you know it. Of course you would care. You're just letting yourself off the hook."

"Oh my God, she's looking this way. Look at that smile. Those lips ..."

"That's it, I'm done trying to help you," said Chris. "You're on your own – and by the way – I don't want to hear another thing about red lips, long legs or green eyes. You want to talk to me about a woman, it better be about Lizzie and that's it."

"Fine by me," I said, thankful that I could have my own thoughts and fantasies without Chris' interruptions and attempts at logic.

~~~~~~~~

"Hi, ready to go?" asked Leah.

"Definitely, I'll just finish this when we get back," I said. I looked over at Chris and smiled. He just looked at me and shook his head. Our friendship has definitely cooled off the past few weeks.

Lunch was great. The food was delicious and the conversation was amazing, as I had always thought it would be. We talked and laughed, and we lost track of time. Two hours later, we returned to work. We apologized to the right people, and were quickly forgiven. Well, not by everyone. Chris was cold as ice. He was on the phone when I returned. I heard him whisper, "He's back. I'll see you tonight at dinner. Love you."

"Who were you talking to Chris? Were you talking about me?"

"I was talking to my wife, you know, the one I'm faithful to, the one I don't keep secrets from. Remember those days, when you didn't have anything to hide?"

"Forget it, you're just jealous I had lunch with a gorgeous woman."

"No, I am absolutely *not* jealous. I have a gorgeous woman waiting for me at home." Chris turned and started working on his computer, ignoring me the rest of the afternoon. I didn't believe him. He was jealous, he just didn't want to admit it.

~~~~~~~~

"Hi honey, some of the guys are going out for a drink after work, so I'll be home late. That's okay, right? Okay, see you later. Bye."

Chris looked over at me briefly, knowing I was lying to my wife. He didn't look happy but didn't say anything. I wonder how much he has told Rachel about what's going on. Hopefully, he's keeping his mouth shut. He'd better.

"We're ready to go, are you ready?" asked Leah, putting on a coat.

"I'm just shutting down my computer, but I'm ready," I say.

"Want to join us, Chris?" asked Leah.

"My wife is waiting for me, so, no thanks," he said.

"Well, have a good night then," she said with a smile.

The next day I couldn't stop smiling. I was still reeling from the night before. I felt like I could walk on water, so energized, so free.

Chris gave me the daggers all day, and wouldn't speak to me. His loss. I know he's jealous, he just won't admit it.

~~~~~~~~

There was a knock on our office wall. I turned and saw Leah standing in the doorway. "We need to talk," she said.

89

"Sure, let's go in the conference room," I said. She wasn't smiling, and instantly I became nervous.

"I just found out I'm being transferred to the Denver office. It's a Vice President position and I can't turn it down. This is what I've been working so hard for. I can't say no."

"What about us?" I asked.

"Come on, you know this wasn't going anywhere. We both have families. I love my husband, and he's excited for a life in Denver."

"You've already told him?"

"Of course! I called him right away. Matt wanted an answer as soon as possible. Did you think I would talk to you about it before my husband?"

"Well, quite frankly, yes. I mean, what we've been doing, what we've shared these past few weeks, doesn't that mean anything to you?"

"Of course it does, but it's not reality. It's fantasy. You and I, we meet for great sex, it's not real life. We escape our responsibilities for a couple hours here and there and it's fun, but that's all it is. I thought you felt the same way. I'm surprised that you thought more was going on."

I went back to my desk. I couldn't believe she broke things off with me. I risked everything to be with her, and I even lost my friendship with Chris. We were friends for over twenty years.

"Want to have lunch today?" I asked Chris.

"No thanks," he replied, not even looking up at me.

"I'd like to talk to you," I said. "I need a friend right now."

"No," said Chris. "I *was* a friend to you. A good one that tried to talk you out of this foolishness, and now that she's ended things with you, you want your friend back, when the past few weeks you couldn't give a shit about me. Like I said, no thanks."

"How do you know she ended things?" I asked.

"Are you for real? You haven't talked to me in weeks.

Now all of a sudden she needs to talk to you, and now you need to talk to me. Of course she ended it. I can't believe you thought it was a permanent thing. I've heard she's being transferred. Ever think that she'll find another fling out there? Ever thought about how many flings she's had in the past? How can you fall for someone like that? Well, I guess it was easy for you, since you're now the same way. I feel sorry for Lizzie and the kids, but certainly not for you. Leave me alone, I have to finish my quarterly reports."

"If that's the way you want it," I said.

"None of this is the way I wanted it, believe me," said Chris, not looking up from his computer.

I sat down and got to work myself. Suddenly, the realization of what I had done had begun to sunk in. I looked at the picture on my desk of Lizzie and the kids. My eyes started to water. *What have I done?*

I sat at my desk, staring at the computer monitor. Chris was right. I was living in a fantasy world. Leah was fun and exciting. Lizzie was real life and responsibility. Leah and I were always on our best behavior, of course we never fought, because there was nothing real between us. I looked at the picture again. *How could I do this to her?* She has given me everything – my life, my family, my true happiness.

I went online and found the number of a local florist. I picked up the phone and dialed. "Yes, I would like a dozen red roses delivered to my wife, please. Can those be delivered this afternoon? Great."

I glanced over at Chris and he was looking at me. He didn't say anything, and I was thankful.

"I've been a fool," I said. He simply nodded and looked back at his computer screen.

# The Violin

"Hey, honey? Remember a little while ago you asked what you could do while I was golfing with the guys?"

"Of course I do, it was just a few minutes ago."

"Well, looks like the new neighbors are having a yard sale. Come take a look."

"Huh, well look at that. Maybe I'll go introduce myself, since I wasn't home on their move-in day."

"Sounds like a great idea to me. Well, I'm off. I'm meeting everyone for breakfast before we golf."

"Have fun, and tell the guys I said hello. Who knows, maybe I'll find something interesting over there."

"You never know, right? See you later."

"See you later."

As I looked amongst the treasures, I found a couple pieces of nice furniture for the sun porch and the study, but what really caught my eye was a violin case.

"Do you play?" a pleasant woman asked.

"No, but I've always wanted to. How old is this thing?"

"I have no idea. It was left behind I guess. I found it in the attic. When I contacted the previous owner they said it wasn't theirs. It was hidden in a corner, I guess they didn't even know it was there."

"I'm Melissa, nice to meet you. I live across the street over there, in the blue house."

"Oh, yes. We met your husband the day we moved in. I'm Holly. Holly Morrison."

"Nice to meet you. I'm just so intrigued by this violin. It looks so old, doesn't it? How much do you want for it?"

"How about ten dollars?" asked Holly.

"I'll take it. Even if I never learn to play it, there's just something about it, I have to have it."

"Well, in that case, twenty dollars!"


The first thing I did when I got home was set the case on a towel on the kitchen table. I opened the case and there sat a very old violin. I bet it used to be a beautiful instrument.

I went online and googled "violins Cleveland Ohio" to see what I could find. The first result was Stearns Violins. I scrolled down a little bit and came across "Violins of Hope – Cleveland, OH." I clicked on this. A man named Amnon Weinstein founded Violins of Hope. He actually restores violins from the Holocaust. I read through the entire website. I was fascinated.

I picked up the violin to look at it closer. Something inside me decided right there I was going to learn how to play it – after I had it restored that is. I turned it over to look at the back. I heard something inside. There was a piece of paper, folded into a small square. I could see it, but how am going to get it out of there? I ran up to the bathroom and got some tweezers. It took a long time, but I managed to get the paper out. I couldn't believe it!

The paper was yellowed, the writing in pencil faded, but I could still make out what it said. Before reading it, I took a picture of it – both with my camera and the camera on my phone. My phone is always with me, and for some reason, I wanted this note near me as well. It read:

*"My name is Simon Abramowitz. I am 19 years old. I am from Poland, and this is my violin. This instrument has so far, saved my life. I hope it brings joy to many after my certain death here at Auschwitz. I play it day and night. It is*

*supposed to calm the new arrivals. As if they don't know what is going to happen to them. But I play it still, to stay alive one more day. 10-8-41*

I immediately called the number for Amnon Weinstein's Violins of Hope in the hope that he would speak to me and look at this note and violin. It was now my new dream that he would restore it and someone would play it in remembrance of Simon, and so many others like Simon.

I have heard about and read about the Holocaust my entire life. I knew the second I saw this old beat up violin case that it was something special, it truly spoke to me, and now, perhaps thanks to Violins of Hope, it will be played again, in honor of all those who lost their lives, needlessly.

# Happy Place

Everyone has a happy place. Where is yours? What place makes you so happy you could cry when you arrive there?

The first time I saw St. John, I was on a cruise. The actual stop was St. Thomas, but we took a ferry to St. John. It was our wedding day, and I couldn't believe the beauty I saw all around me. I had never felt so relaxed and so at home as I did on this island.

Hawks Nest Beach was where the wedding ceremony took place. There were five of us on the entire beach. Lynne and Joe, our witnesses, and Anne Marie Porter, our minister.

It was a beautiful ceremony under an arch of branches. After we said our "I dos" Rick ran through the water with his suit on, it was quite funny. We were so excited that day, but most of all we loved where we were, and we promised we would be back soon.

We have kept that promise, because we have been to St. John, either by cruise or by staying there a week, almost every year since we were married. Every time we go we learn something more and discover something new about the island.

All of the beaches are beautiful, but I think our favorite is Cinnamon Bay – the beach Kenny Chesney writes about in his songs. Then there is Trunk Bay, which is a State Park, also beautiful and great for snorkeling. Salt Pond Bay is a little bit of a hike to get to, but beautiful once you get there.

To sit on the beach, underneath arches of bushes, looking at the beautiful blue water, seeing the sunny sky, I am definitely in my happy place. It's fun to people-watch, read a good book, journal my thoughts, go for a swim, or just close your eyes and listen to the ocean and laughter of children.

Our favorite place to eat on the island is "Skinny Legs." I love the name of it! Friendly people, good music, outdoor atmosphere and delicious food. We go there every time we're there.

There are places to shop of course, but we head right for the beaches every time.

Never before has a place made me feel like St. John does. If we were ever to win the lottery I know we would live there permanently. For now, we'll enjoy our annual visits and I will daydream of my happy place.

# Who Rescued Who

When we made the heartbreaking decision to take our 13 ½ year old Pekingese, Maggie, to the vet for the last time, we were devastated. She brought us so much joy for so many years, it was the least we could do to hold her and be with her until the end. We cried the entire time, and the vet told us that Maggie's body was shutting down; she made the decision for us. We said goodbye to her and I sang "You are my sunshine" to her until she took her last breath.

When we got in the car, I said "Never again, no more dogs. There is no way I can go through that again. My husband agreed. We spent the afternoon running errands so we didn't have to go home to the empty house.

When we finally got home, the silence was deafening. Maggie had such a presence, and even after she went blind she still greeted us at the door. There was no one to meet us at the door that day, and it made me cry all over again. Seeing her toys around the house, her little bed that she never slept in broke my heart. I didn't know how I was going to get through this, and neither did my husband. Maggie was really "my" dog, but he loved her too.

The next day I arrived at work with bloodshot eyes from crying during the whole commute, and walking into my office to see a picture of Maggie didn't help at all. Somehow, I managed to get through the work day. Every day was this way for the rest of the week.

The following Sunday morning, while I was at breakfast with my husband, I blurted out, "I can't stand the silence, we need to get another dog."

"Oh, thank God," said Rick. "I totally agree." That day we started our search online. We knew we wanted to get a rescue dog, so we looked at some sites. So many dogs were available for adoption! We looked and looked until Rick came across a photo of a little Chihuahua mix named Rownie. She was *adorable*! In the photograph she fit in the palm of a girl's hand. She had big brown eyes, and dark fur. We kept looking at her. I'm not going to say it was love at first sight, but I knew she was pretty special.

I downloaded the application and also attached a letter telling Dixie Underground Pet Rescue our story, how we had lost Maggie but had a lot of love to give another dog.

The following day I got a call from Beth at Dixie Underground. She was calling to talk about Rownie and do a phone interview with me. The conversation went really well, and our adoption was approved! In about a month, when Rownie reached 12 weeks of age, we would pick her up in Connecticut and bring her home!

"I would like to change her name," I said to Rick.

"Okay, what should we call her?" he asked.

"I'd like to name her Isabel, after Maggie's mother. What do you think?"

"I think that's a great idea," he said. For the first time in a long time, I smiled, and I meant it.

~~~~~~~~

"Are you ready to go?" I asked Rick. It was early, about 4:00 a.m. We were meeting "Pooches on the Move" at 7:00 a.m. in Connecticut. Thank goodness it was all highway driving, she would be easy to find.

We reached the rest stop and "Pooches on the Move" hadn't arrived yet. There were quite a few other people there waiting also.

After a little while, we saw a white van pull into the parking lot.

*This is it! She's finally here.* I couldn't help but wonder, will I feel guilty for loving this dog?  Is it too soon after Maggie?  It's only been six weeks since Maggie passed away. *I guess we'll see.*

Dogs started coming out of the van and given to their new owners. There were dogs of all sizes, some were excited and some were clearly scared. Still no sign of Isabel, but we were waiting patiently.

All of a sudden I heard someone say, "Come on, Rownie, it's okay. Come on."  She wouldn't come out of the van. The driver climbed into the van for a few minutes. She came back out with a little tiny bundle of fur that was clearly shaking, poor thing. There she was, our little girl. She was so adorable, but I felt bad that she was so scared. The driver went to hand her to me and Isabel started to pee!  She was one scared little girl. We put her on the ground so she could finish for a minute.

When she was done, I picked her up and held her. Still shaking, she looked up at me with her big brown eyes. She had such a pretty face.

Rick and I brought her to the car, and she stayed in my lap the entire ride home. She spent a lot of the ride looking up at me so I talked to her and rubbed her back. Eventually, she stopped shaking.

After a few hours, we arrived home, and when we entered our house, I put her on the floor so she could wander around and look at her new home. She seemed to like it! I gave her some new toys, and she immediately started to play with a squeaky toy shaped like a cow we call "MooMoo." I put down some water, dry food and some moist food too. She didn't seem to like the moist food so we gave her some deli turkey – she gobbled it right up! To this day, she loves deli turkey. We don't like to call her "spoiled," we call her "well-loved."

It wasn't long before little Isabel got comfortable in her new home and made some new (human) friends. She has added so much joy to our lives in such a short time. She's the sweetest dog I've ever met, very affectionate. I've never seen a dog that likes to kiss the way she does!

I am so grateful that we found her and brought her into our home. We will always remember Maggie, but Isabel has now made our family complete.

Yes, she's a rescue dog, but she rescued us right back!

# Last Thoughts

I was about thirteen years old when I started using drugs. It started out simple, drinking beer and some hard stuff like vodka. That turned into cigarettes, and that turned into marijuana and that turned into heroin, my drug of choice. I had my first kid when I was fifteen, but I traded her for a fix. I'm not sure where she is now, or the son I had four years after that, but I'm sure they're okay. They must be, they're not with me.

I'll admit, drugs are the most important thing in my life, it's my full time job really, to stay high. In the past twenty-six years I've had five kids, and none of them are with me. Some live with their grandparents I've heard and doing real well. Can't ask for better than that I guess. Technically, I'm homeless, but I've never slept on the streets. I spend my nights with whoever will have me – usually the person who gives me my nightly fix. I guess you think I'm a whore or something, and well, I suppose you're right.

I spend a lot of time at the ocean. The salty air clears my mind, as much as it can be cleared. I'm sitting here on a huge rock looking out at the water, and things are so clear right now, in this moment. I have regrets, they crash on me like the waves would if I were in the water. I think of my kids, and try to remember their ages. I think they're something like 26, 19, 17, 16 and 12. Something like that. I'm trying to remember the months of their birthdays, I know some are in the summer, and two are in the springtime. My first one, I think she was a winter baby, a lot has happened since then.

I think of the life they would have had if I kept them with me. I know they are better off wherever they are. I'm glad they are doing well. I'm sure they're being taken care of, by someone.

There isn't much I can do for them anyway, I'm sitting here, on this rock, there is a needle hanging from my arm, and everything that was so clear a minute ago is all blurry and confusing. This will be my last hit I think. I'm pretty sure I took too much. No one will miss me. I haven't done enough in my life to be missed, I'm smart enough to know that but too stupid to do anything about it. Over the years, people have tried to help me, straighten out and sober up. But the drugs, they're a part of me, I just can't stop. I wish my kids and my family were enough to make me want to stop but I'm a selfish woman so they're just not. I know that's horrible, I know this is the end, and maybe that will be my gift to everyone, to not be here, to not burden anyone, to no longer live my life from one fix to the next. The moonlight looks beautiful on the dark water. The sound of the waves and the smell of the salt, that's what is guiding me home, away from this terrible life I've made for myself. I'm glad it's almost over, I really am.

# Not What I Expected

I was thirty-three years old when I was diagnosed with Rapid Cycling Bipolar Disorder. Honestly, I always knew there was something wrong with me but I had no idea what it was. I was always quite moody, very sensitive, terrible with money, and always felt a little out of place.

Bipolar Disorder is a psychological disorder often associated with disruptive and extreme mood swings alongside fluctuating energy levels as well. These episodes of elation and depression are very different from the normal peak of emotions that regular people experience in their daily lives. The term bipolar is actually derived from these people's tendency to shift from one extreme mood polarity to the other almost instantly during manic-depressive episodes. Another name for this condition is manic depression and manic depressive disorder, and is often related to consecutive episodes of hypomania and depression. Rapid-cycling has to do with the frequency of episodes. At least four episodes occur annually and sometimes within a span of several days or sometimes even within the same day. I'd say I have an episode of either manic or depressive every week to some level.

Having this disorder is not an easy life, that's for sure. On what I call "normal days" I'm pretty much the same as regular people especially when it comes to moods and emotions. However, it gets a little complicated when something triggers a manic depressive attack my mood either goes extremely high or plummets, almost successively. It can either be mild hypomania or a mild case of the blues but extremes can cause loss of interest in everyday activities which can make me feel unstable and even suicidal. A long time ago I would have hallucinations. I couldn't distinguish realty from fantasy.

Mania or hypomania is the extreme high mood and emotional levels, often characterized by feelings of euphoria or elation. During a manic episode, a bipolar person feels very confident, almost invincible. Self-esteem becomes bloated and I feel like I can do anything. This is when making sound decisions becomes tricky, almost impossible.

In a manic episode I talk much faster than I usually do, and sometimes I just say whatever comes to mind. My thoughts are disorganized and I feel the need to rush to get things done, sometimes multiple things, which is more than I can handle.

Also in a manic episode I tend to spend money on things I don't need or even want. It's so hard to focus and concentrate, making work difficult. I remember the first time I was hospitalized one of the nurses tried to get me to fill out paperwork to receive disability compensation. I said "I'm not disabled," and refused.

During depression episodes, I hit rock bottom. I feel so hopeless, useless and infinitely sad – for *no reason*. Suicidal thoughts have taken over a few times, but again, not for a long time. Also during depression I have a very hard time sleeping, feel anxious, and guilty – over nothing – and everything. I feel like everything bad that happens is my fault. Ridiculous, right?

Yet another thing that happens for me during depression is binge eating or I stop eating completely. Don't look to me to pay attention to you much during this time either, because I can't focus on anything but my sadness. I become angry, annoyed and irritated at trivial things. I have skipped out on social situations and work during these episodes as well.

To make things even more confusing, sometimes mania and depression are mixed, meaning I have both at the same time. When I said living with this disorder isn't easy, I meant it.

In researching my condition I have learned that bipolar can be passed genetically. In my case, this makes sense. I was adopted at eight months old. The only thing I know about my birth mother is that she was thirty-three years old and married. In 1968, I can't imagine it was common that a married woman would give up her baby – not without a darn good reason. Maybe she was bipolar, and couldn't take care of me. I'll never know for sure, obviously, but to think this way makes sense to me.

Neurological makeup can be another factor. This means bipolar comes from the way the brain is structured. There have been studies that show that brain structures and processes are different from "regular people."

I have even read that development in bipolar children follows a pattern that is very similar to that of schizophrenia. Abnormal brain patterns are commonly linked to the dramatic changes in the mood of a bipolar person.

Hormonal substances in the brain and the nervous system can be responsible for the development of bipolar disorder. Hormones play an important role in brain processes, and if something goes wrong with them then it could result in a manic or depressive episode.

Again, I don't know exactly how or why this is part of my life, but I try my best to live with it. I take my medication every day, which makes me feel like a "normal person" most of the time.

There are times, though, where there are triggers – stress, seasonal changes, lack of sleep, food intake are all triggers for me. Stressful events, such as the death of a loved one, or my fear of heights, or getting lost in a strange place – these push me over the edge. My manic episodes seem to happen more often during the spring and summer, and depression happens mostly during the winter. Lack of sleep takes place during manic episodes because my mind races like crazy. It's important for me to have a regular sleep schedule – and a routine in general. I do better with a structured routine which makes being spontaneous a little challenging. Sugar-induced mania has happened to me a few times, and it's always followed by a huge plummet of emotion. Not easy.

I think bipolars get a bad rap, especially on television. Bipolars are different than psychopaths. Some bipolars commit crimes during a hallucinatory episode and a lot of bipolars, such as myself, are highly functioning. I have a full-time job in a law office as a legal assistant, I'm a writer, I'm a wife, a mother, a sister, a daughter, a friend, a co-worker, I'm active in my church and my faith is strong. I'm happy to say that I share the title of being bipolar with Ludwig Van Beethoven.

I owe a lot of my success as a person to my family. They have been so supportive through the years since my diagnosis – which by the way – took place two months after I got married. Poor Rick, I'm sure this isn't what he expected. It's not what he signed up for, but he has stuck by me through the years and does his best to be supportive through all my moods. Another reason I'm successful is because of my medication. I couldn't function without it, and even though it took a while to find the right medication, my days are normal, and that makes me happy.

I think of my days that I spent in hospitals, when I was at my absolute lowest, and I am so thankful for the people who helped me there and the other patients that I met. Those are unforgettable days for sure.

I think of all the highs and lows I've experienced, all the medications I've tried, all the emotions I've felt, how hard I've worked with meeting all my responsibilities such as work, driving, dealing with finances, housework, and my personal relationships with God, with my family and friends, and even strangers. This is not an easy life I live, there is a stigma and it can be pretty lonely, but I know I'm not alone with this condition, I've got great support systems. I've also gotten really good at monitoring my moods and knowing the signs and possible triggers. I'm also really good at using my coping mechanisms when I need them. I do things that help me relax, such as writing, reading, watching television, playing with my dog, spending time with my family and my friends and sticking to my daily routines.

I want to thank my family and friends for walking this walk with my, I know it can't be easy, but thanks to you it's a little easier for me to live with.